My Congr[...]

"Presents" Series and to its

Readers —

May the Romance live on!

With my very best wishes

Penny Jordan

Dear Reader,

I'm delighted to be part of the twenty-fifth birthday celebration of Harlequin Presents®! My very first Presents was published twelve years ago. Since then, I've had the pleasure of meeting some of you and of hearing from many others. You and I have a lot in common. We both love exciting heroes, strong heroines and stories that make us laugh and cry. My warmest thanks to you for enjoying my books, and my best wishes to Presents. May we all celebrate many more birthdays together!

With love,

Sandra Marton

P.S. Look out next month for *The Divorcee Said Yes!*, the second funny, tender and exciting tale in my new series of three terrific stories, THE WEDDING OF THE YEAR.

SANDRA MARTON

The Bride Said Never!

THE WEDDING OF THE YEAR

Harlequin Books

TORONTO • NEW YORK • LONDON
AMSTERDAM • PARIS • SYDNEY • HAMBURG
STOCKHOLM • ATHENS • TOKYO • MILAN
MADRID • WARSAW • BUDAPEST • AUCKLAND

ISBN 0-373-11955-0

THE BRIDE SAID NEVER!

First North American Publication 1998.

CHAPTER ONE

DAMIAN SKOURAS did not like weddings.

A man and a woman, standing before clergy, friends and family while they pledged vows of love and fidelity no human being could possibly keep, was the impossible stuff of weepy women's novels and fairy tales.

It was surely not reality.

And yet, here he was, standing in front of a flower-bedecked altar while the church organ shook the rafters with Mendelssohn's triumphal march and a hundred people oohed and ahhed as a blushing bride made her way up the aisle toward him.

She was, he had to admit, quite beautiful, but he knew the old saying. All brides were beautiful. Still, this one, regal in an old-fashioned gown of white satin and lace and clutching a bouquet of tiny purple and white orchids in her trembling hands, had an aura about her that made her more than beautiful. Her smile, just visible through her sheer, fingertip-length veil, was radiant as she reached the altar.

Her father kissed her. She smiled, let go of his arm, then looked lovingly into the eyes of her waiting groom, and Damian sent up a silent prayer of thanks to the gods of his ancestors that it was not he.

It was just too damned bad that it was Nicholas, instead.

Beside him, Nicholas gave a sudden, unsteady lurch. Damian looked at the young man who'd been his ward until three years ago. Nick's handsome face was pale.

Damian frowned. "Are you all right?" he murmured.

Nick's adam's apple bobbed up and down as he swallowed. "Sure."

It's not too late, boy, Damian wanted to say, but he knew

5

better. Nick was twenty-one; he wasn't a boy any longer. And it *was* too late, because he fancied himself in love.

That was what he'd said the night he'd come to Damian's apartment to tell him that he and the girl he'd met not two months before were getting married.

Damian had been patient. He'd chosen his words carefully. He'd enumerated a dozen reasons why marrying so quickly and so young were mistakes. But Nick had a ready answer for every argument, and finally Damian had lost his temper.

"You damned young fool," he'd growled, "what happened? Did you knock her up?"

Nick had slugged him. Damian almost smiled at the memory. It was more accurate to say that Nick had tried to slug him but at six foot two, Damian was taller than the boy, and faster on his feet, even if Nicholas was seventeen years younger. The hard lessons he'd learned on the streets of Athens in his boyhood had never quite deserted him.

"She's not pregnant," Nick had said furiously, as Damian held him at arm's length. "I keep telling you, we're in love."

"Love," Damian had said with disdain, and the boy's eyes had darkened with anger.

"That's right. Love. Dammit, Damian, can't you understand that?"

He'd understood, all right. Nick was in lust, not love; he'd almost told him so but by then he'd calmed down enough to realize that saying it would only result in another scuffle. Besides, he wasn't a complete fool. All this arguing was only making the boy more and more determined to have things his own way.

So he'd spoken calmly, the way he assumed his sister and her husband would have done if they'd lived. He talked about Responsibility and Maturity and the value in Waiting a Few Years, and when he'd finished, Nick had grinned and said yeah, he'd heard that stuff already, from both of Dawn's parents, and while that might be good advice for some, it had nothing to do with him or Dawn or what they felt for each other.

Damian, who had made his fortune by knowing not just when to be aggressive but when to yield, had gritted his teeth, accepted the inevitable and said in that case, he wished Nick well.

Still, he'd kept hoping that either Dawn or Nick would come to their senses. But they hadn't, and now here they all were, listening to a soft-voiced clergyman drone on and on about life and love while a bunch of silly women, the bride's mother included, wept quietly into their hankies. And for what reason? She had been divorced. Hell, *he* had been divorced, and if you wanted to go back a generation and be foolish enough to consider his parents' marriage as anything but a farce, they were part of the dismal breakup statistics, too. Half the people here probably had severed marriages behind them including, for all he knew, the mealymouthed clergyman conducting this pallid, non-Greek ceremony.

All this pomp and circumstance, and for what? It was nonsense.

At least his own memorable and mercifully brief foray into the matrimonial wars a dozen years ago had never felt like a real marriage. There'd been no hushed assembly of guests, no organ music or baskets overflowing with flowers. There'd been no words chanted in Greek nor even the vapid sighing of a minister like this one.

His wedding had been what the tabloids called a quickie, an impulsive flight to Vegas after a weekend spent celebrating his first big corporate takeover with too much sex and champagne and not enough common sense. Unfortunately he'd made that assessment twenty-four hours too late. The quickie marriage had led to a not-so-quickie divorce, once his avaricious bride and a retinue of overpriced attorneys had gotten involved.

So much for the lust Nick couldn't imagine might masquerade as love.

A frown appeared between Damian's ice-blue eyes. This was hardly the time to think about such things. Perhaps a miracle would occur and it would all work out. Perhaps, years from now, he'd look back and admit he'd been wrong.

Lord, he hoped so.

He loved Nick as if he were his own flesh and blood. The boy was the son he'd never had and probably never would have, given the realities of marriage. That was why he'd agreed to stand here and pretend to be interested in the mumbo jumbo of the ceremony, to smile at Nick and even to dance with the plump child who was one of the bridesmaids and treat her with all the kindness he could manage because, Nick had said, she was Dawn's best friend and not just overweight but shy, too, and desperately afraid of being a wallflower at the reception afterward.

Oh, yes, he would do all the things a surrogate father was supposed to do. And when the day ended, he'd drive to the inn on the lake where he and Gabriella had stayed the night before and take her to bed.

It would be the best possible way to get over his disappointment at not having taught Nick well enough to protect him from the pain that surely lay ahead, and it would purge his mind of all this useless, sentimental claptrap.

Damian looked at his current mistress, seated in a pew in the third row. Gabriella wasn't taken in by any of it. Like him, she had tried marriage and found it not to her liking. Marriage was just another word for slavery, she'd said, early in their relationship...though lately, he'd sensed a change. She'd become less loving, more proprietorial. "Where have you been, Damian?" she'd say, when a day passed without a phone call. She'd taken his move to a new apartment personally, too; he'd only just in time stopped her from ordering furniture for him as a "surprise."

She hadn't liked that. Her reaction had been sharp and angry; there'd been a brittleness to her he'd never seen before—though today, she was all sweetness and light.

Even last night, during the rehearsal, there'd been a suspicious glint in her dark brown eyes. She'd looked up and smiled at him. It had been a tremulous smile. And, as he'd watched, she'd touched a lace handkerchief to her eyes.

Damian felt a twinge of regret. Perhaps it was time to move on. They'd had, what, almost six months together but when a woman got that look about her...

"Damian?"

Damian blinked. Nicholas was hissing at him out of the side of his mouth. Had the boy come to his senses and changed his mind?

"The ring, Damian!"

The ring. Of course. The best man was searching his pockets frantically, but he wouldn't find it. Nick had asked Damian to have it engraved and he had, but he'd forgotten to hand it over.

He dug in his pocket, pulled out the simple gold band and dropped it into Nick's outstretched hand. Across the narrow aisle, the maid of honor choked back a sob; the bride's mother, tears spilling down her cheeks, reached for her ex-husband's hand, clutched it tightly, then dropped it like a hot potato.

Ah, the joys of matrimony.

Damian forced himself to concentrate on the minister's words.

"And now," he said, in an appropriately solemn voice, "If there is anyone among us who can offer a reason why Nicolas Skouras Babbitt and Dawn Elizabeth Cooper should not be wed, let that person speak or forever—"

Bang!

The double doors at the rear of the church flew open and slammed against the whitewashed walls. There was a rustle of cloth as the guests shifted in the pews and turned to see what was happening. Even the bride and groom swung around in surprise.

A woman stood in the open doorway, silhouetted against the sunlight of the spring afternoon. The wind, which had torn the doors from her hands, ruffled her hair wildly around her head and sent her skirt swirling around her thighs.

A murmur of shocked delight spread through the church. The minister cleared his throat.

The woman stepped forward, out of the brilliance of the light and into the shadowed interior. The excited murmur of voices, which had begun to die away, rose again.

And no wonder, Damian thought. The latecomer was incredibly beautiful.

She looked familiar, but surely if he'd met her before, he'd know her name. A man didn't forget a woman who looked like this.

Her hair was the color of autumn, a deep auburn shot with gold, and curled around her oval, high-cheekboned face. Her eyes were widely spaced and enormous. They were...what? Gray, or perhaps blue. He couldn't tell at this distance. She wore no jewelry but then, jewelry would only have distracted from her beauty. Even her dress, the color of the sky just before a storm, was simple. It was a shade he'd always thought of as violet but the fashion police surely had a better name for it. The cut was simple, too: a rounded neckline, long, full sleeves and a short, full skirt, but there was nothing simple about the body beneath the dress.

His gaze slid over the woman, taking in the high, rounded breasts, the slim waist, the gentle curve of her hips. She was a strange combination of sexuality and innocence, though the innocence was certainly manufactured. It had to be. She was not a child. And she was too stunning, too aware of herself, for it not to be.

Another gust of wind swept in through the open doors. She clutched at her skirt but not before he had a look at legs as long and shapely as any man's dream, topped by a flash of something black and lacy.

The crowd's whispers grew louder. Someone gave a silvery laugh. The woman heard it, he was certain, but instead of showing embarrassment at the attention she was getting, she straightened her shoulders and her lovely face assumed a look of disdain.

I could wipe that look from your face, Damian thought suddenly, and desire, as hot and swift as molten lava, flooded his veins.

Oh, yes, he could. He had only to stride down the aisle, lift her into his arms and carry her out into the meadow that unrolled like a bright green carpet into the low hills behind the church. He'd climb to the top of those hills, lay her down in the soft grass, drink the sweetness of her mouth while he undid the zipper on that pale violet dress and then taste every inch of her as he kissed his way down her body. He imagined burying himself between her thighs and entering her, moving within her heat until she cried out in passion.

Damian's mouth went dry. What was the matter with him? He was not a randy teenager. He wasn't given to fantasizing about women he didn't know, not since he'd been, what, fifteen, sixteen years old, tucked away in his bed at night, breathing heavily over a copy of a men's magazine.

This was nonsense, he thought brusquely, and just then, the woman's head lifted. She looked directly up the aisle, her gaze unwavering as it sought his. She stared at him while his heartbeat raced, and then she smiled again.

I know what you're thinking, her smile said, and I find it terribly amusing.

Damian heard a roaring in his ears. His hands knotted at his sides; he took a step forward.

"Damian?" Nick whispered, and just at that minute, the wind caught the doors again and slammed them against the whitewashed walls of the old church.

The sound seemed to break the spell that had held the congregants captive. Someone cleared a throat, someone else coughed, and finally a man in the last pew rose from his seat, made his way to the doors and drew them shut.

He smiled pleasantly at the woman, as if to say there, that's taken care of, but she ignored both the man and the smile as she looked around for the nearest vacant seat. Slipping into it, she crossed those long legs, folded her hands in her lap and assumed an expression of polite boredom.

What, she seemed to ask, was the delay?

The minister cleared his throat. Slowly, almost reluctantly, the congregants turned and faced the altar.

"If there is no one present who can offer a reason why Nicolas and Dawn should not be wed," he said briskly, as if fearing another interruption, "then, in accordance with the laws of God and the State of Connecticut, I pronounce them husband and wife."

Nick turned to his bride, took her in his arms and kissed her. The organist struck a triumphant chord, the guests rose to their feet and Damian lost sight of the woman in a blur of faces and bodies.

Saved by the bell, Laurel thought, though it was more accurate to say she'd been saved by a C major chord played on an organ.

What an awful entrance to have made! It was bad enough she'd arrived late for Dawn's wedding, but to have interrupted it, to have drawn every eye to her...

Laurel swallowed a groan.

Just last week, during lunch, Dawn had predicted that was exactly what would happen.

Annie had brought her daughter to New York for the final fitting on her gown, and they'd all met for lunch at Tavern on the Green. Dawn, with all the drama in her eighteen-year-old heart, had looked at Laurel and sighed over her Pasta Primavera.

"Oh, Aunt Laurel," she'd said, "you are so beautiful! I wish I looked like you."

Laurel had looked across the table at the girl's lovely face, innocent of makeup and of the rough road that was life, and she'd smiled.

"If *I* looked like *you*," she'd said gently, "I'd still be on the cover of *Vogue*."

That had turned the conversation elsewhere, to Laurel's declining career, which Annie and Dawn stoutly insisted wasn't declining at all, and then to Laurel's plans for the future, which she'd managed to make sound far more exciting than they so far were.

And, inevitably, they'd talked about Dawn's forthcoming wedding.

"You are going to be the most beautiful bride in the world," Laurel had said, and Dawn had blushed, smiled and said well, she certainly hoped Nick would agree, but that the most beautiful woman at the wedding would undoubtedly be her aunt Laurel.

Laurel had determined in that moment that she would not, even inadvertently, steal the spotlight. When you had a famous face—well, a once-famous face, anyway—you could do that just by entering a room, and that was the last thing she wanted to do to the people she loved.

So this morning, she'd dressed with that in mind. Instead of the pale pink Chanel suit she'd bought for the occasion, she'd put on a periwinkle blue silk dress that was a couple of years old. Instead of doing her hair in the style that she'd made famous—whisked back and knotted loosely on the crown, with sexy little curls tumbling down her neck—she'd simply run a brush through it and let it fall naturally around her shoulders. She hadn't put on any jewelry and she'd even omitted the touch of lip gloss and mascara that was the only makeup she wore except when she was on a runway or in front of a camera.

She'd even left early, catching a train at Penn Station that was supposed to have gotten her into Stratham a good hour before the ceremony was scheduled to begin. But the train had broken down in New Haven and Laurel had started to look for a taxi when the station public address system announced that there'd be a new train coming along to pick up the stranded passengers in just a few minutes.

The clerk at the ticket counter confirmed it, and said the train would be lots faster than a taxi.

And so she'd waited, for almost half an hour, only to find that it wasn't a train that had been sent to pick up the passengers at all. It was a bus and, of course, it had taken longer than the train ever would have, longer than a taxi would have, too, had she taken one when the train had first ground to a halt. The icing on the cake had come when they'd finally reached Stratham and for endless minutes, there hadn't been a cab in sight.

"Aunt Laurel?"

Laurel looked up. Dawn and her handsome young groom had reached her row of pews.

"Baby," she said, fixing a bright smile to her face as she reached out and gave the girl a quick hug.

"That was some entrance," Dawn said, laughing.

"Oh, Dawn, I'm so sorry about—"

Too late. The bridal couple was already moving past her, toward the now-open doors and the steps that led down from the church.

Laurel winced. Dawn had been teasing, she knew, but Lord, if she could only go back and redo that awful entrance.

As it was, she'd stood outside the little church after the cab had dropped her off, trying to decide which was preferable, coming in late or missing the ceremony, until she'd decided that missing the ceremony was far worse. So she'd carefully cracked the doors open, only to have the wind pull them from her hands, and the next thing she'd known she'd been standing stage-center, with every eye in the place on her.

Including his. That man. That awful, smug-faced, egotistical man.

Was he Nicholas's guardian? Well, former guardian. Damian Skouras, wasn't that the name? That had to be him, considering where he'd been standing.

One look, and she'd known everything she needed to

know about Damian Skouras. Unfortunately she knew the type well. He had the kind of looks women went crazy for: wide shoulders, narrow waist, a hard body and a handsome face with eyes that seemed to blaze like blue flame against his olive skin. His hair swept back from his face like the waves on a midnight sea, and a tiny gold stud glittered in one ear.

Looks and money, both, Laurel thought bitterly. It wasn't just the Armani dinner jacket and black trousers draped down those long, muscled legs that had told her so, it was the way he held himself, with careless, masculine arrogance. It was also the way he'd looked at her, as if she were a new toy, all gift-wrapped and served up for his pleasure. His smile had been polite but his eyes had said it all.

"Baby," those eyes said, "I'd like to peel off that dress and see what's underneath."

Not in *this* lifetime, Laurel thought coldly.

She was tired of it, sick of it, if the truth were told. The world was filled with too many insolent men who'd let money and power go to their heads.

Hadn't she spent almost a year playing the fool for one of them?

The rest of the wedding party was passing by now, bridesmaids giggling among themselves in a pastel flurry of blues and pinks, the groomsmen grinning foolishly, impossibly young and good-looking in their formal wear. Annie went by with her ex and paused only long enough for a quick hug after which Laurel fell back into the crowd, letting it surge past her because she knew *he'd* be coming along next, the jerk who'd stared at her and stripped her naked with his eyes...and yes, there he was, bringing up the rear of the little procession with one of the bridesmaids, a child no more than half his age, clinging to his arm like a limpet.

The girl was staring up at him with eyes like saucers while he treated her to a full measure of his charm, smiling at her with his too-white teeth glinting against his too-tanned skin. Laurel frowned. The child was positively transfixed by the body-by-health club, tan-by-sunlamp and attitude-by-bank-balance. And Mr. Macho was eating up the adulation.

Bastard, Laurel thought coldly, eyeing him through the crowd, and before she had time to think about it, she stepped out in the aisle in front of him.

The bridesmaid was so busy making goo-goo eyes at her dazzling escort that she had to skid to a stop when he halted.

"What's the matter?" the girl asked.

"Nothing," he answered, his eyes never leaving Laurel's.

The girl looked at Laurel. Young as she was, awareness glinted in her eyes.

"Come on, Damian. We have to catch up to the others."

He nodded. "You go on, Elaine. "I'll be right along."

"It's Aileen."

"Aileen," he said, his eyes still on Laurel. "Go ahead. I'll be just behind you."

The girl shot Laurel a sullen glare. "Sure." Then she picked up her skirts and hurried along after the others.

Close up, Laurel could see that the man's eyes were a shade of blue she'd never seen before, cool and pale, the irises as black-ringed as if they'd been circled with kohl. Ice, she thought, chips of polar sea ice.

A pulse began to pound in her throat. I should have stayed where I was, she thought suddenly, instead of stepping out to confront him…

"Yes?" he said.

His voice, low and touched with a slight accent, was a perfect match for the chilly removal of his gaze.

The church was empty now. A few feet away, just beyond the doors, Laurel could hear the sounds of laughter but here, in the silence and the lengthening shadows of late afternoon, she could hear only the *thump-thump* of her heart.

"Was there something you wished to say to me?"

His words were polite but the coldness in them made Laurel's breath catch. For a second, she thought of turning and running but she'd never run from anything in her life. Besides, why should she let this stranger get the best of her?

There was nothing to be afraid of, nothing at all.

So she drew herself up to her full five foot ten, tossed her hair back from her face and fixed him with a look of cool *hauteur*, the same one she wore like a mask when she was on public display, and that had helped make her a star on runways from here to Milan.

"Only that you look pathetic," she said regally, "toying with that little girl."

"Toying with…?"

"Really," she said, permitting her voice to take on a purr of amusement, "don't you think you ought to play games with someone who's old enough to recognize you for what you are?"

The man looked at her for a long moment, so long that she foolishly began to think she'd scored a couple of points. Then he smiled in a way that sent her heart skidding up into her throat and he stepped forward, until he was only a hand's span away.

"What is your name?"

"Laurel," she said, "Laurel Bennett, but I don't see—"

"I agree completely, Miss Bennett. The game is far more enjoyable when it is played by equals."

She saw what was coming next in his eyes, but it was too late. Before Laurel could move or even draw back, he reached out, took her in his arms and kissed her.

CHAPTER TWO

LAUREL SHOT a surreptitious glance at her watch.

Another hour, and she could leave without attracting attention. Only another hour—assuming she could last that long.

The man beside her at the pink-and-white swathed table for six, Evan Something-or-Other, was telling a joke. Dr. Evan Something-or-Other, as Annie, ever the matchmaker, had pointedly said, when she'd come around earlier to greet her guests.

He was a nice enough man, even if his pink-tipped nose and slight overbite did remind Laurel of a rabbit. It was just this was the doctor's joke number nine or maybe nine thousand for the evening. She'd lost count somewhere between the shrimp cocktail and the *Beouf aux Chanterelles*.

Not that it mattered. Laurel would have had trouble keeping her mind on anything this evening. Her thoughts kept traveling in only one direction, straight towards Damian Skouras, who was sitting at the table on the dais with an expensively dressed blond windup doll by his side—not that the presence of the woman was keeping him from watching Laurel.

She knew he was, even though she hadn't turned to confirm it. There was no need. She could feel the force of his eyes on her shoulder blades. If she looked at him, she half expected to see a pair of blue laser beams blazing from that proud, arrogant face.

The one thing she *had* confirmed was that he was definitely Damian Skouras, and he was Nicholas's guardian. Former guardian, anyway; Nick was twenty-one, three years past needing to ask anyone's permission to marry. Laurel knew that her sister hadn't wanted the wedding to take place. Dawn and Nick were too young, she'd said. Laurel had kept her own counsel but now that she'd met the man who'd raised Nick, she was amazed her sister hadn't raised yet a second objection.

Who would want a son-in-law with an egotistical SOB like Damian Skouras for a role model?

That was how she thought of him, as an Egotistical SOB, and in capital letters. She'd told him so the next time she'd seen him, after that kiss, when they'd come face-to-face on the receiving line. She'd tried breezing past him as if he didn't exist, but he'd made that impossible, capturing her hand in his, introducing himself as politely as if they'd never set eyes on each other until that second.

Flushed with indignation, Laurel had tried to twist her hand free. That had made him laugh.

"Relax, Miss Bennett," he'd said in a low, mocking tone. "You don't want to make another scene, do you? Surely one such performance a day is enough, even for you."

"I'm not the one who made a scene, you—you—"

"My name is Damian Skouras."

He was laughing at her, damn him, and enjoying every second of her embarrassment.

"Perhaps you enjoy attracting attention," he'd said. "If so, by all means, go on as you are. But if you believe, as I do, that today belongs to Nicholas and his bride, then be a good girl, smile prettily and pretend you're having a good time, hmm?"

He was right, and she knew it. The line had bogged down behind her and people were beginning to crane their necks with interest, trying to see who and what was holding things up. So she'd smiled, not just prettily but brilliantly, as if she were on a set instead of at a wedding, and said, in a voice meant to be heard by no one but him, that she was hardly surprised he still thought it appropriate to address a woman as a girl and that she'd have an even better time if she pretended he'd vanished from the face of the earth.

His hand had tightened on hers and his eyes had glinted with a sudden darkness that almost made her wish she'd kept her mouth shut.

"You'll never be able to pretend anything when it comes to me," he'd said softly, "or have you forgotten what happened when I kissed you?"

Color had shot into her face. He'd smiled, let her snatch her hand from his, and she'd swept past him.

No, she hadn't forgotten. How could she? There'd been that first instant of shocked rage and then, following hard on its heels, the dizzying realization that she was suddenly clinging to his broad shoulders, that her mouth was softening and parting under his, that she was making a little sound in the back of her throat and moving against him...

"...well," Evan Something-or-Other droned, "if that's the case, said the chicken, I guess there's not much point crossing to the other side!"

Everybody at the table laughed. Laurel laughed, too, if a beat too late.

"Great story," someone chuckled.

Evan smiled, lifted his glass of wine, and turned to Laurel.

"I guess you heard that one before," he said apologetically.

"No," she said quickly, "no, I haven't. I'm just—I think it must be jet lag. I was in Paris just yesterday and I don't think my head's caught up to the clock." She smiled. "Or vice versa."

"Paris, huh? Wonderful city. I was there last year. A business conference."

"Ah."

"Were you there on business? Or was it a vacation?"

"Oh, it was business."

"I guess you're there a lot."

"Well…"

"For showings. That's what they call them, right?"

"Well, yes, but how did you—"

"I recognized you." Evan grinned. "Besides, Annie told me. I'm her dentist, hers and Dawn's, and the last time she came by for a checkup she said, 'Wait until you meet my baby sister at the wedding. She's the most gorgeous model in the world.'" His grin tilted. "But she was wrong."

"Was she?" Laurel asked, trying to sound interested. She knew what came next. If the doctor thought this was a new approach, he was sadly mistaken.

"Absolutely. You're not the most gorgeous model in the world, you're the most gorgeous woman, hands down."

Drum roll, lights up, Laurel thought, and laughed politely. "You'll have to forgive Annie. She's an inveterate matchmaker."

"At least she didn't exaggerate." He chuckled and leaned closer. "You should see some of the so-called 'dream dates' I've been conned into."

"This isn't a date, Doctor."

His face crumpled just a little and Laurel winced. There was no reason to let her bad mood out on him.

"I meant," she said with an apologetic smile, "I know what you're saying. I've been a victim of some pretty sneaky setups, myself."

"Matchmakers." Evan shook his head. "They never let up, do they? And I wish you'd call me 'Evan'"

"Evan," Laurel said. "And you're right, they never do."

"Annie wasn't wrong, though, was she?" Evan cleared his throat. "I mean, you are, ah, uninvolved and unattached?"

Annie, Laurel thought wearily, what am I going to do with you? Her sister had been trying to marry her off for years. She'd really gone into overdrive after Laurel had finally walked out on Kirk.

"Okay," Annie had said, "so at first, you didn't want to settle down because you had to build your career. Then you convinced yourself that jerk would pop the question, but, big surprise, he didn't.''

"I don't want to talk about it," Laurel had replied, but Annie had plowed on, laying out the joys of matrimony as if she hadn't untied her own marriage vows years before, and eventually Laurel had silenced her by lying through her teeth and saying that if the right man ever came along, she supposed she'd agree to tie the knot....

But not in this lifetime. Laurel's mouth firmed. So far as she could see, the only things a woman needed a man for was to muscle open a jar and provide sex. Well, there were gizmos on the market that dealt with tight jar lids. As for sex…it was overrated. That was something else she'd learned during her time with Kirk. Maybe it meant more to women who didn't have careers. Maybe there was a woman somewhere who heard music and saw fireworks when she was in bed with a man but if you had a life, sex was really nothing more than a biological urge, like eating or drinking, and certainly not anywhere near as important.

"Sorry," Evan said, "I guess I shouldn't have asked."

Laurel blinked. "Shouldn't have…?

"If you were, you know, involved."

"Oh." She cleared her throat. "Oh, no, don't apologize. I'm, ah, I'm flattered you'd ask. It's just that, well, what with all the traveling I do—"

"Miss Bennett?"

Laurel stiffened. She didn't have to turn around to know who'd come up behind her. Nobody could have put such a world of meaning into the simple use of her name—nobody but Damian Skouras.

She looked up. He was standing beside her chair, smiling pleasantly.

"Yes?" she said coldly.

"I thought you might like to dance."

"You thought wrong."

"Ah, but they're playing our song."

Laurel stared at him. For the most part, she'd been ignoring the band. Now, she realized that a medley of sixties hits had given way to a waltz.

"Our sort of song, at any rate," Damian said. "An old-fashioned waltz, for an old-fashioned girl." His smile tilted. "Sorry. I suppose I should say 'woman.'"

"You suppose correctly, Mr. Skouras. Not that it matters. Girl or woman, I'm not interested."

"In waltzing?"

"Waltzing is fine." Laurel's smile was the polite equal of his. "It's you I'm not interested in, on the dance floor or off it."

Across the table, there was a delighted intake of breath. Every eye had to be on her now and she knew it, but she didn't care. Not anymore. Damian Skouras had taken this as far as she was going to allow.

"You must move in very strange circles, Miss Bennett. In my world, a dance is hardly a request for an assignation."

Damn the man! He wasn't put off by what she'd said, or even embarrassed. He was amused by it, smiling first at her and then at the woman who'd gasped, and somehow managing to turn things around so that it was Laurel who looked foolish.

It wasn't easy, but she managed to dredge up a smile.

"And in mine," she said sweetly, "a man who brings his girlfriend to a party and then spends his time hitting on another woman is called a—"

"Hey," a cheerful voice said, "how's it going here? Everybody having a good time?"

Laurel looked over her shoulder. The bride and groom had come up on her other side and were beaming at the tableful of guests.

"Yes," someone finally said, after some throat-clearing, "we're having a splendid time, Nicholas."

"Great. Glad to hear it." Nick grinned. "One thing I learned, watching the ladies set up the seating chart, is that you never know how these table arrangements are going to work out.'' He looked at Laurel, then at Damian, and his grin broadened. ''Terrific! I see that you guys managed to meet on your own.''

The woman opposite Laurel made a choked sound and lifted her napkin to her lips.

Damian nodded. ''We did, indeed,'' he said smoothly.

Dawn leaned her head against her groom's shoulder. ''We just knew you two would have a lot to talk about.''

I don't believe this, Laurel thought. *I'm trapped in a room filled with matchmakers.*

''Really,'' she said politely.

''Uh-huh.''

''Name one thing.''

Dawn's brows lifted. ''Sorry?''

''Name one thing we'd have to talk about,'' Laurel said pleasantly, even while a little voice inside her warned her it was time to shut up.

The woman across the table made another choking sound. Dawn shot Nick a puzzled glance. Gallantly he picked up the slack.

''Well,'' he said, ''the both of you do a lot of traveling.''

''Indeed?''

''Take France, for instance.''

''France?''

''Yeah. Damian just bought an apartment in Paris. We figured you could clue him in on the best places to buy stuff. You know, furniture, whatever, considering that you spend so much time there.''

''I don't,'' Laurel said quickly. She looked at Evan, sitting beside her, and she cleared her throat. ''I mean, I don't spend half as much time in Paris as I used to.''

''Where do you spend your time, then?'' Damian asked politely.

Where didn't he spend his? Laurel made a quick mental inventory of all the European cities a man like this would probably frequent.

"New York," she said, and knew instantly it had been the wrong choice.

"What a coincidence," Damian said with a little smile. "I've just bought a condominium in Manhattan."

"You said it was Paris."

"Paris, Manhattan..." His shoulders lifted, then fell, in an elegant shrug. "My business interests take me to many places, Miss Bennett, and I much prefer coming home to my own things at night."

"Like the blonde who came with you today?" Laurel said sweetly.

"Aunt Laurrr-el!" Dawn said, with a breathless laugh.

"It's quite all right, Dawn," Damian said softly, his eyes on Laurel's. "Your aunt and I understand each other— don't we, Miss Bennett?"

"Absolutely, Mr. Skouras." Laurel turned to the dentist, who was sitting openmouthed, a copy of virtually everyone else at the table. "Would you like to dance, Evan?"

A flush rose on his face. He looked up at Damian.

"But—I mean, I thought..."

"You thought wrong, sir." Damian's tone was polite but Laurel wasn't fooled. Anger glinted in his eyes. "While we've all been listening to Miss Bennett's interesting views, I've had the chance to reconsider." He turned to Dawn and smiled pleasantly. "My dear, I would be honored if you would desert Nicholas long enough to grant me the honor of this dance."

Dawn smiled with relief. "I'd be thrilled."

She went into his arms at the same time Laurel went into Evan's. Nick pulled out Evan's chair, spun it around and sat down. He draped his arms over the back and made some light remark about families and family members that diverted the attention of the others and set them laughing.

So much for Damian Skouras, Laurel thought with satisfaction as she looked over Evan's shoulder. Perhaps next time, he'd think twice before trying to play what were certainly his usual games with a woman.

*   *   *

Gabriella Boldini crossed and recrossed her long legs under the dashboard of Damian's rented Saab.

"Honestly, Damian," she said crossly, "I don't know why you didn't arrange for a limousine."

Damian sighed, kept his attention focused on the winding mountain road and decided there was no point in responding to the remark she'd already made half a dozen times since they'd left Stratham.

"We'll be at the inn soon," he said. "Why don't you put your head back and try and get some sleep?"

"I am not tired, Damian, I'm simply saying—"

"I know what you're saying. You'd have preferred a different car."

Gabriella folded her arms. "That's right."

"A Cadillac, or a Lincoln, with a chauffeur."

"Yes. Or you could have had Stevens drive us up here. There's no reason we couldn't have been comfortable, even though we're trapped all the way out in the sticks."

Damian laughed. "We're hardly in the 'sticks', Gaby. The inn's just forty miles from Boston."

"For goodness' sakes, must you take me so literally? I know where it is. We spent last night there, didn't we?" Gabriella crossed her legs again. If the skirt of her black silk dress rode any higher on her thighs, Damian thought idly, it would disappear. "Which reminds me. Since that place doesn't have room service—"

"It has room service."

"There you go again, taking me literally. It doesn't have room service, not after ten o'clock at night. Don't you remember what happened when I tried to order a pot of tea last night?"

Damian's hands flexed on the steering wheel. "I remember, Gaby. The manager offered to brew you some tea and bring it up to our suite himself."

"Nonsense. I wanted herbal tea, not that stuff in a bag. And I've told you over and over, I don't like it when you call me Gaby."

What the hell is this? Damian thought wearily. He was not married to this woman but anyone listening to them now would think they'd been at each other's throats for at least a decade of blissful wedlock.

Not that a little sharp-tongued give-and-take wasn't sometimes amusing. The woman at Nicholas's wedding, for instance. Laurel Bennett had infuriated him, at the end, doing her damnedest to make him look foolish in front of Nicholas and all the others, but he had to admit, she was clever and quick.

"'Gaby' always makes me think of some stupid character in a bad Western."

She was stunning, too. The more he'd seen of her, the more he'd become convinced he'd never seen a more exquisite face. She was a model, Dawn had told him, and he'd always thought models were androgynous things, all bones and no flesh, but Laurel Bennett had been rounded and very definitely feminine. Had that been the real reason he'd asked her to dance, so he could hold that sweetly curved body in his arms and see for himself if she felt as soft as she looked?

"Must you drive so fast? I can barely see where we're going, it's so miserably dark outside."

Damian's jaw tightened. He pressed down just a little harder on the gas.

"I like to drive fast," he said. "And since I'm the one at the wheel, you don't have to see outside, now do you?"

He waited for her to respond, but not even Gabriella was that foolish. She sat back instead, arms still folded under her breasts, her head lifted in a way he'd come to know meant she was angry.

The car filled with silence. Damian was just beginning to relax and enjoy it when she spoke again.

"Honestly," she said, "you'd think people would use some common sense."

Damian shot her a quick look. "Yes," he said, grimly, "you would."

"Imagine the nerve of that woman."

"What woman?"

"The one who made that grand entrance. You know, the woman with that mass of dyed red hair."

Damian almost laughed. Now, at least, he knew what this was all about.

"Was it dyed?" he asked casually. "I didn't think so."

"You wouldn't," Gabriella snapped. "Men never do. You're all so easily taken in."

We are, indeed, he thought. What had happened to Gabriella's sweet nature and charming Italian accent? The first had begun disappearing over the past few weeks; the second had slipped away gradually during the past hour.

"And that dress. Honestly, if that skirt had been any shorter..."

Damian glanced at Gabriella's legs. Her own skirt, which had never done more than flirt with the tops of her thighs, had vanished along with what was left of her pleasant disposition and sexy accent.

"She's Dawn's aunt, I understand."

"Who?" Damian said pleasantly.

"Don't be dense." Gabriella took a deep breath. "That woman," she said, more calmly, "the one with the cheap-looking outfit and the peroxide hair."

"Ah," he said. The turnoff for the inn was just ahead. He slowed the car, signaled and started up the long gravel driveway. "The model."

"Model, indeed. Everyone knows what those women are like. That one, especially." Gabriella was stiff with indignation. "They say she's had dozens of lovers."

The car hit a rut in the road. Damian, eyes narrowed, gave the wheel a vicious twist.

"Really," he said calmly.

"Honestly, Damian, I wish you'd slow—"

"What else do they say about her?"

"About...?" Gabriella shot him a quick glance. Then she reached forward, yanked down the sun visor and peered into the mirror on its reverse side. "I don't pay attention to gossip," she said coolly, as she fluffed her fingers through her artfully arranged hair. "But what *is* there to say about someone who poses nude?"

A flash fire image of Laurel Bennett, naked and flushed in his bed, seared the mental canvas of Damian's mind. He forced himself to concentrate on the final few yards of the curving road.

"Nude?" he said calmly.

"To all intents and purposes. She did an ad for Calvin Klein—it's in this month's *Chic* or maybe *Femme*, I'm not sure which." Gabriella snapped the visor back into place. "Oh, it was all very elegant and posh, you know, one of those la-di-da arty shots taken through whatever it is they use, gauze, I suppose." Her voice fairly purred with satisfaction. "She'd need it, wouldn't she, seeing that she's a bit long in the tooth? Still, gauze or no gauze, when you came right down to it, there she was, stark naked."

The picture of Laurel burned in his brain again. Damian cleared his throat. "Interesting."

"Cheap is a better word. Totally cheap...which is why I just don't understand what made you bother with her."

"You're talking nonsense, Gabriella."

"I saw the way you looked at her and let me tell you, I didn't much like it. You have an obligation to me."

Damian pulled up at the entrance to the inn, shut off the engine and turned toward her.

"Obligation?" he said carefully.

"That's right. We've been together for a long time now. Doesn't that mean anything to you?"

"I have not been unfaithful to you."

"That's not what I'm talking about and you know it." She took a deep breath. "Can you really tell me you sat through that entire wedding without feeling a thing?"

"I felt what I always feel at weddings," he said quietly. "Disbelief that two people should willingly subject themselves to such nonsense along with the hope, however use-

less, that they make a success of what is basically an un-
natural arrangement.''

Gabriella's mouth thinned. ''How can you say such a
thing?''

''I say it because it's true. You knew that was how I felt,
from the start. You said your attitude mirrored mine.''

''Never mind what I said,'' Gabriella said sharply. ''And
you haven't answered my question. Why did you keep
looking at that woman?''

*Because I chose to. Because you don't own me. Because
Laurel Bennett intrigues me as you never did, not even
when our affair first began.*

Damian blew out his breath. It was late, they were both
tired and this wasn't the time to talk or make decisions. He
ran his knuckles lightly over Gabriella's cheek, then
reached across her lap and opened her door.

''Go on,'' he said gently. ''Wait in the lobby while I
park the car.''

''You see what I mean? If we'd come by limousine, you
wouldn't have to drop me off here, in the middle of nowhere. But no, you had to do things your way, with no
regard for me or my feelings.''

Damian glanced past Gabriella, to the brightly lit entrance to the inn. Then he looked at his mistress's face,
illuminated by the cruel fluorescent light that washed into
the car, and saw that it wasn't as lovely as he'd once
thought, especially not with petulance and undisguised jeal-
ousy etched into every feature.

''Gaby,'' he said quietly, ''it's late. Let's not argue about
this now.''

''Don't think you can shut me up by sounding sincere,
Damian. And I keep telling you, my name's not Gaby!''

A muscle knotted in his jaw. He reached past her again,
grasped the handle, slammed the door closed and put the
Saab in gear.

''Wait just a minute! I'm not going with you while you
park the car. If you think I have any intention of walking

through that gravel in these shoes..." Gabriella frowned as Damian pulled through the circular driveway and headed downhill. "Damian? What are you doing?"

"What does it look like I'm doing?" He kept his eyes straight ahead, on the road. "I'm driving to New York."

"Tonight? But it's late. And what about my things? My clothes and my makeup? Damian, this is ridiculous!"

"I'll phone the inn and tell them to pack everything and forward it, as soon as I've dropped you off."

"Dropped me off?" Gabriella twisted toward him. "What do you mean? I never go back to my own apartment on weekends, you know that."

"What you said was true, a few minutes ago," he said, almost gently, "I do have an obligation to you." He looked across the console at her, then back at the road. "An obligation to tell you the truth, which is that I've enjoyed our time together, but—"

"But what? What is this, huh? The big brush-off?"

"Gabriella, calm down."

"Don't you tell me to calm down," she said shrilly. "Listen here, Mr. Skouras, maybe you can play high-and-mighty with the people who work for you but you can't pull that act with me!"

"I'd like us to end this like civilized adults. We both knew our relationship wouldn't last forever."

"Well, I changed my mind! How dare you toss me aside, just because you found yourself some two-bit—"

"I've found myself nothing." His voice cut across hers, harsh and cold. "I'm simply telling you that our relationship has run its course."

"That's what *you* think! What *I* think is that you led me to have certain expectations. My lawyer says..."

Gabriella stopped in midsentence, her mouth opening and closing as if she were a fish, but it was too late. Damian had already pulled onto the shoulder of the road. He swung toward her, and she shrank back in her seat at the expression on his face.

"Your lawyer says?" His voice was low, his tone dangerous. "You mean, you've already discussed our relationship with an attorney?"

"No. Well, I mean, I had a little chat with—look, Damian, I was just trying to protect myself." In the passing headlights of an oncoming automobile, he could see her face harden. "And it looks as if I had every reason to! Here you are, trying to dump me without so much as a by-your-leave—"

Damian reached out and turned on the radio. He punched buttons until he found a station playing something loud enough to drown out Gabriella's voice. Then he swung back onto the road and stepped down, hard, on the gas.

Less than three hours later, they were in Manhattan. Sunday night traffic was sparse, and it took only minutes for him to reach Gabriella's apartment building on Park Avenue.

The doorman hurried up. Gabriella snarled at him to leave her alone as she stepped from the car.

"Bastard," she hissed, as Damian gunned the engine.

For all he knew, she was still staring after him and spewing venom as he drove off. Not that it mattered. She was already part of the past.

CHAPTER THREE

JEAN KAPLAN had been Damian Skouras's personal assistant for a long time.

She was middle-aged, happily married and dedicated to her job. She was also unflappable. Nothing fazed her.

Still, she couldn't quite mask her surprise when her boss strode into the office Monday morning, said a brisk, "Hello," and then instructed her to personally go down to the newsstand on the corner and purchase copies of every fashion magazine on display.

"Fashion magazines, Mr. Skouras?"

"Fashion magazines, Ms. Kaplan." Damian's expression was completely noncommittal. "I'm sure you know the sort of thing I mean. *Femme, Chic*...all of them."

Jean nodded. "Certainly, sir."

Well, she thought as she hurried to the elevator, her boss had never been anyone's idea of a conventional executive. She permitted herself a faint smile as the doors whisked open at the lobby level. When you headed up what the press loved to refer to as the Skouras Empire, you didn't have to worry about that kind of thing.

Maybe he was thinking of buying a magazine. Or two, or three, she thought as she swept up an armload of glossy publications, made her way back to her employer's thirtieth floor office and neatly deposited them on his pale oak desk.

"Here you are, Mr. Skouras. I hope the assortment is what you wanted."

Damian nodded. "I'm sure it is."

"And shall I send the usual roses to Miss Boldini?"

He looked up and she saw in his eyes a flash of the Arctic

coldness that was faced by those who were foolish enough to oppose him in business.

"That won't be necessary."

"Oh. I'm sorry, sir. I just thought…"

"In fact, if Miss Boldini calls, tell her I'm not in."

"Yes, sir. Will that be all?"

Damian's dark head was already bent over the stack of magazines.

"That's all. Hold my calls until I ring you, please."

Jean nodded and shut the door behind her.

So, she thought with some satisfaction, Gabriella Boldini, she of the catlike smile and claws to match, had reached the end of her stay. Not a minute too soon, as far as she was concerned. Jean had seen a lot of women flounce through her employer's life, all of them beautiful and most of them charming or at least clever enough to show a pleasant face to her. But Gabriella Boldini had set her teeth on edge from day one.

Jean settled herself at her desk and turned on her computer. Perhaps that was why Mr. Skouras had wanted all those magazines. He'd be living like a monk for the next couple of months; he always did, after an affair ended. What better time to research a new business venture? Soon enough, though, another stunning female would step into his life, knowing she was just a temporary diversion but still hoping to snare a prize catch like him.

They always hoped, even though he never seemed to know it.

Jean gave a motherly sigh. As for herself, she'd given up hoping. There'd been a time she'd clung to the belief that her boss would find himself a good woman to love. Not anymore. He'd had one disastrous marriage that he never talked about and it had left him a confirmed loner.

Amazing, how a man so willing to risk everything making millions could refuse to take any risks at all, in matters of the heart.

*   *   *

Damian frowned as he looked over the magazines spilling across his desk.

Headlines screamed at him.

Are You Sexy Enough to Keep Your Man Interested?
Ten Ways to Turn Him On
Sexy Styles for Summer
The Perfect Tan Starts Now

Was there really a market for such drivel? He'd seen Gabriella curled up in a chair, leafing through magazines like these, but he'd never paid any attention to the print on the covers.

Or to the models, he thought, his frown deepening as he leafed through the glossy pages. Why did so many of them look as if they hadn't eaten in weeks? Surely, no real man could find women like these attractive, with their bones almost protruding through their skin.

And those pouting faces. He paused, staring at an emaciated-looking waif with a heavily made-up face who looked up from the page with an expression that made her appear to have sucked on one lemon too many.

Who would find such a face attractive?

After a moment, he sighed, closed the magazine and reached for another. Laurel's photograph wasn't where Gabriella had said it would be. Not that it mattered. There'd been no good reason to want to see the picture; he'd directed his secretary to buy these silly things on a whim.

Come on, man, who are you kidding?

It hadn't been a whim at all. The truth was that he'd slept poorly, awakening just after dawn from a fragmented dream filled with the kinds of images he hadn't had in years, his loins heavy and aching with need...

And there it was. The photograph of Laurel Bennett.

Gabriella had been wrong. Laurel wasn't nude, and he

tried to ignore the sense of relief that welled so fiercely inside him at the realization.

She'd been posed with her back to the camera, her head turned, angled so that she was looking over her shoulder at the viewer. Her back and shoulders were bare; a long length of ivory silk was draped from her hips, dipping low enough to expose the delicate tracery of her spine almost to its base. Her hair, that incredible mane of sun-streaked mahogany, tumbled over her creamy skin like tongues of dark flame.

Damian stared at the picture. All right, he told himself coldly, there she is. A woman, nothing more and nothing less. Beautiful, yes, and very desirable, but hardly worth the heated dreams that had disturbed his night.

He closed the magazine, tossed it on top of the others and carried the entire stack to a low table that was part of a conversational grouping at the other end of his office. Jean could dispose of them later, either toss them out or give them to one of the clerks. He certainly had no need for them, nor had he any further interest in Laurel Bennett.

That was settled, then. Damian relaxed, basking in the satisfaction that came of closure.

His morning was filled with opportunities for that same feeling, but it never came again.

There was a problem with a small investment firm Skouras International had recently acquired. Damian's CPAs had defined it but they hadn't been able to solve it. He did, during a two-hour brainstorming session. A short while later, he held a teleconference with his bankers in Paris and Hamburg, and firmed up a multimillion dollar deal that had been languishing for months.

At twenty of twelve, he began going through the notes Jean had placed on a corner of his desk in preparation for his one o'clock business luncheon, but he couldn't concentrate. Words kept repeating themselves, and entire sentences.

He gave up, pushed back his chair and frowned.

Suddenly he felt restless.

He rose and paced across the spacious room. There was always a carafe of freshly brewed coffee waiting for him on a corner shelf near the sofas that flanked the low table where he'd dumped the magazines.

He paused, frowning as he looked down at the stack. The magazine containing Laurel's photo was on top and he picked it up, opened it to that page and stared at the picture. Her hair looked like silk. Would it feel that way, or would it be stiff with hair spray when he touched it, the way Gabriella's had always been? How would her skin smell, when he put his face to that graceful curve where her shoulder and her neck joined? How would it taste?

Hell, what was the matter with him? He wasn't going to smell this woman, or taste her, or touch her.

His eyes fastened on her face. There was a hands-off coolness in her eyes that seemed at odds with her mouth, which looked soft, sexy, and heart-stoppingly vulnerable. It had felt that way, too, beneath his own, after she'd stopped fighting the passion that suddenly had gripped them both and given herself up to him, and to the kiss.

His belly knotted as he remembered the heat and hardness that had curled through his body. He couldn't remember ever feeling so caught up in a kiss or in the memory of what had been, after all, a simple encounter.

So caught up, and out of control.

Damian's jaw knotted. This was ridiculous. He was never out of control.

What he had, he thought coldly, was an itch, and it needed scratching.

One night, and that would be the end of it.

He could call Laurel, ask her to have drinks or dinner. It wouldn't be hard; he had learned early on that information was easy to come by, if you knew how to go about getting it.

She was stubborn, though. Her response to him had been fiery and he knew she wanted him as badly as he wanted her, but she'd deny it. He looked down at the ad again. She'd probably hang up the phone before he had the chance to—

A smile tilted at the corner of his mouth. Until this minute, he hadn't paid any attention to the advertisement itself. If pressed, he'd have said it was for perfume, or cosmetics. Perhaps furs.

Now he saw just how wrong he'd have been. Laurel was offering the siren song to customers in the market for laptop computers. And the company was one that Skouras International had bought only a couple of months ago.

Damian reached for the phone.

Luck was with him. Ten minutes later, he was in his car, his luncheon appointment canceled, forging through midday traffic on his way to a studio in Soho, where the next in the series of ads was being shot.

"Darling Laurel," Haskell said, "that's not a good angle. Turn your head to the right, please."

Laurel did.

"Now tilt toward me. Good."

What was good about it? she wondered. Not the day, surely. Not what she was doing. Why did everything, from toothpaste to tugboats, have to be advertised with sex?

"A little more. Yes, like that. Could you make it a bigger smile, please?"

She couldn't. Smiling didn't suit her mood.

"Laurel, baby, you've got to get into the swing of things. You look utterly, totally bored."

She *was* bored. But that was better than being angry. Don't think about it anymore, she told herself, just don't think about it.

Or him.

"Ah, Laurel, you're starting to scowl. Bad for the face, darling. Relax. Think about the scene. You're on the deck of a private yacht in, I don't know, the Aegean."

"The Caribbean," she snapped.

"What's the matter, you got something against the Greeks? Sure. The Caribbean. Whatever does it for you. Just get into it, darling. There you are, on a ship off the coast of Madagascar."

"Madagascar's in Africa."

"Jeez, give me a break, will you? Forget geography, okay? You're on a ship wherever you want, you're stretched out in the hot sun, using your Redwood laptop to write postcards to all your pals back home."

"That's ridiculous, Haskell. You don't write postcards on a computer."

Haskell glared at her. "Frankly, Laurel, I don't give a flying fig what you're using that thing for. Maybe you're writing your memoirs. Or tallying up the millions in your Swiss bank account. Whatever. Just get that imagination working and give us a smile."

Laurel sighed. He was right. She was a pro, this was her job, and that was all there was to it. Unfortunately she'd slept badly and awakened in a foul mood. It didn't help that she felt like a ninny, posing in a bikini in front of a silly backdrop that simulated sea and sky. What did bikinis, sea and sky have to do with selling computers?

"Laurel, for heaven's sake, I'm losing you again. Concentrate, darling. Think of something pleasant and hang on to it. Where you're going to have supper tonight, for instance. How you spent your weekend. I know it's Monday, but there's got to be something you can imagine that's a turn-on."

Where she was having supper tonight? Laurel almost laughed. At the kitchen counter, that was where, and on the menu was cottage cheese, a green salad and, as a special treat, a new mystery novel with her coffee.

As for how she'd spent the weekend—if Haskell only knew. That was the last thing he'd want her to think about.

To think she'd let Damian Skouras humiliate her like that!

"Hey, what's happening? Laurel, babe, you've gone

from glum to grim in the blink of an eye. Come on, girl.
Grab a happy thought and hang on.''

A happy thought? A right cross, straight to Damian
Skouras's jaw.

"Good!"

A knee, right where it would do the most good.

"Great!" Haskell began moving around her, his camera
at his eye. "Hold that image, whatever it is, because it's
working."

A nice, stiff-armed jab into his solar plexus.

"Wonderful stuff, Laurel. That's my girl!"

Why hadn't she done it? Because there'd already been
too many eyes on them, that was why. Because if she'd
done what she'd wanted to do, she'd have drawn the attention of everyone in the room, to say nothing of ruining
Dawn's day.

"Look up, darling. That's it. Tilt your head. Good. This
time, I want something that smolders. A smile that says
your wonderful computer's what's made it possible for you
to be out here instead of in your office, that in a couple of
minutes you'll leave behind this glorious sun and sea,
traipse down to the cabin and tumble into the arms of a
gorgeous man." Haskell leaned toward her, camera whir-
ring. "You do know a gorgeous man, don't you?"

Damian Skouras.

Laurel stiffened. Had she said the words aloud? No,
thank goodness. Haskell was still dancing around her, his
eye glued to his camera.

Damian Skouras, gorgeous? Don't be silly. Men weren't
"gorgeous."

But he was. That masculine body. That incredible face,
with the features seemingly hewn out of granite. The eyes
that were a blue she'd never seen before. And that mouth,
looking as if it had been chiseled from a cold slab of marble
but instead feeling warm and soft and exciting as it took
hers.

"Now you've got it!" Haskell's camera whirred and

clicked until the roll of film was done. Then he dumped
the camera on his worktable and held out his hand. "Baby,
that was great. The look on your face..." He sighed dramatically. "All I can say. is, wow!"

Laurel put the computer on the floor, took Haskell's
hand, rose to her feet and reached for the terry-cloth robe
she'd left over the back of a chair.

"Are we finished?"

"We are, thanks to whatever flashed through your head
just now." Haskell chuckled. "I don't suppose you'd like
to tell me who he was?"

"It wasn't a 'he' at all," Laurel said, forcing a smile to
her lips. "It was just what you suggested. I thought about
what I was having for dinner tonight."

"No steak ever made a woman look like that," Haskell
said with a lecherous grin. "Who's the lucky man, and why
isn't it me?"

"Perhaps Miss Bennett's telling you the truth."

Laurel spun around. The slightly amused male voice had
come from a corner of the cavernous loft, but where? The
brightly lit set only deepened the darkness that lurked in
the corners.

"After all, it's well past lunchtime."

Laurel's heart skipped a beat. No. No, it couldn't be...

Damian Skouras emerged from the shadows like a man
stepping out of the mist.

"Hello, Miss Bennett."

For a minute, she could only gape at this man she'd
hoped never to see again. Then she straightened, drew the
robe more closely around her and narrowed her eyes.

"This isn't funny, Mr. Skouras."

"I'm glad to hear it, Miss Bennett, since comedy's not
my forte."

"Laurel?" Haskell turned toward her. "You know this
guy? I mean, you asked him to meet you here?"

"I do not know him," Laurel said coldly.

Damian smiled. "Of course she knows me. You heard her greet me by name just now, didn't you?"

"I don't know him, and I certainly didn't ask him to meet me here."

Haskell moved forward. "Okay, pal, you heard the lady. This isn't a public gallery. You want to do business with me, give my agent a call."

"My business is with Miss Bennett."

"Hey, what is it with you, buddy? You deaf? I just told you—"

"And I just told you," Damian said softly. He looked at the photographer. "This has nothing to do with you. I suggest you stay out of it."

Haskell's face turned red and he stepped forward. "Who's gonna make me?"

"No," Laurel said quickly, "Haskell, don't."

She knew Haskell was said to have a short fuse and a propensity for barroom brawls. She'd never seen him in action but she'd seen the results, cuts and bruises and once a black eye. Not that Damian Skouras didn't deserve everything Haskell could dish out, but she didn't want him beaten up, not on her account.

She needn't have worried. Even as she watched, the photographer looked into Damian's face, saw something that made him blanch and step back.

"I don't want any trouble in my studio," he muttered.

"There won't be any." Damian smiled tightly. "If it makes you feel better, I have every right to be here. Put in a call to the ad agency, tell them my name and they'll confirm it."

Laurel laughed. "You're unbelievable, do you know that?" She jabbed her hands on her hips and stepped around Haskell. "What will they confirm? That you're God?"

Damian looked at her. "That I own Redwood Computers."

"You're *that* Skouras?" Haskell said.

"I am."

"Don't be a fool, Haskell," Laurel snapped, her eyes locked on Damian's face. "Just because he claims he owns the computer company doesn't mean he does."

"Trust me," Haskell muttered, "I read about it in the paper. He bought the company."

Laurel's chin rose. "How nice for you, Mr. Skouras. That still doesn't give you the right to come bursting in here as if you owned this place, too."

Damian smiled. "That's true."

"It doesn't give you the right to badger me, either."

"I'm not badgering you, Miss Bennett. I heard there was a shoot here today, I was curious, and so I decided to come by."

Laurel's eyes narrowed. "It had nothing to do with me?"

"No," Damian said, lying through his teeth.

"In that case," she said, "you won't mind if I..."

He caught her arm as she started past him. "Have lunch with me."

"No."

"*The Four Seasons*? Or *The Water's Edge*? It's a beautiful day out, Miss Bennett."

"It was," she said pointedly, "until you showed up."

Haskell cleared his throat. "Well, listen," he said, as he backed away, "long as you two don't need me here..."

"Wait," Laurel said, "Haskell, you don't have to..."

But he was already gone. The sound of his footsteps echoed across the wooden floor. A door slammed, and then there was silence.

"Why must you make this so difficult?" Damian said softly.

"I'm not the one making this difficult," Laurel said coldly. She looked down at her wrist, still encircled by his hand, and then at him. "Let go of me, please."

Damian's gaze followed hers. Hell, he thought, what was he doing? This wasn't his style at all. When you came down to it, nothing he'd done since he'd laid eyes on this woman was in character. The way he'd gone after her yesterday, like a bull in rut. And what he'd done moments ago, challenging that photographer like a street corner punk when the man had only been coming to Laurel's rescue. All he'd been able to think, watching the man's face, was, Go on, take your best shot at me, so I can beat you to a pulp.

And that was crazy. He wasn't a man who settled things with his fists. Not anymore; not in the years since he'd worked his way up from summer jobs on the Brooklyn docks to a Park Avenue penthouse.

He wasn't a man who went after a woman with such single-minded determination, either. Why would he, when there were always more women than he could possibly want, ready and waiting to be singled out for his attention?

That was it. That was what was keeping his interest in the Bennett woman. She was uninterested, or playing at being uninterested, though he didn't believe it, not after the way she'd kissed him yesterday. Either way, the cure was the same. Bed her, then forget her. Satisfy this most primitive of urges and she'd be out of his system, once and for all.

But dammit, man, be civilized about it.

Damian let go of her wrist, took a breath and began again.

"Miss Bennett. Laurel. I know we got off to a poor start—"

"You're wrong. We didn't get off to any start. You're playing cat-and-mouse games but as far as I'm concerned, we never even met."

"Well, we can remedy that. Have dinner with me this evening."

"I'm busy."

"Tomorrow night, then."

"Still busy. And, before you ask, I'm busy for the foreseeable future."

He laughed, and her eyes flashed with indignation.

"Did I say something funny, Mr. Skouras?"

"It's Damian. And I was only wondering which of us is pretending what?"

"Which of us..." Color flew into her face. "My God, what an insufferable ego you must have! Do you think this is a game? That I'm playing hard to get?"

He leaned back against the edge of the photographer's worktable, his jacket open and his hands tucked into the pockets of his trousers.

"The thought crossed my mind, yes."

"Listen here, Mr. Skouras..."

"Damian."

"*Mr.* Skouras." Laurel's eyes narrowed. "Let me put this in words so simple even you'll understand. One, I do not like you. Two, I do not like you. And three, I am not interested in lunch. Or dinner. Or anything else."

"Too many men already on the string?"

God, she itched to slap that smug little smile from his face!

"Yes," she said, "exactly. I've got them lined up for mornings, afternoons and evenings, and there're even a couple of special ones I manage to tuck in at teatime. So as you can see, I've no time at all for you in my schedule."

He was laughing openly now, amusement glinting in his eyes, and it was driving her over the edge. She *would* slug him, any second, or punch him in the very center of that oh-so-masculine chest...

Or throw her arms around his neck, drag his head down to hers and kiss him until he swung her into his arms and carried her off into the shadows that rimmed the lighted set...

"Laurel?" Damian said, and their eyes met.

He knew. She could see it in the way he was looking at her. He'd stopped laughing and he knew what she'd thought, what she'd almost done.

"No," she said, and she swung away blindly. She heard him call her name but she didn't turn back, didn't pause.

Moving by instinct, impelled by fear not of Damian but of herself, she ran to the dressing room, flung open the door and then slammed it behind her. She fell back against it and stood trembling, with her heart thudding in her chest.

Outside, in the studio, Damian stood staring at the closed door. His entire body was tense; he could feel the blood pounding through his veins.

She'd been so angry at him. Furious, even more so because he'd been teasing her and she'd known it. And then, all at once, everything had changed. He'd seen the shock of sudden awareness etch into her lovely face and he'd understood it, felt it burn like flame straight into the marrow of his bones.

She'd run not from him but from herself. All he had to do was walk the few feet to the door that sheltered her, open it and take her in his arms. One touch, and she would shatter.

He would have her, and this insanity would be over.

Or would it?

He took a long, ragged breath. She was interesting, this Laurel Bennett, and not only because of the fire that raged under that cool exterior. Other things about her were almost as intriguing. Her ability to play her part in what was quickly becoming a complex game fascinated him, as did her determination to deny what was so obviously happening between them. She was an enigma. A challenge.

Damian smiled tightly. He had not confronted either in a very long time. It was part of the price he'd paid for success.

Perhaps he'd been wrong in thinking that he could get her out of his system by taking her to bed for a long night of passion. Laurel Bennett might prove a diversion that could please him for some time. And he sensed instinctively that, unlike Gabriella, she would not want nor ask for more.

The thought brought another smile to his lips. The women's libbers would hang him from his toes, maybe from a more sensitive part of his anatomy, and burn him in effigy if they ever heard him make such a cool appraisal of a woman, but they'd have been wrong.

He was no chauvinist, he was merely a man accustomed to making intelligent assessments. Laurel was a sophisticated woman who'd had many lovers. Even if Gabriella hadn't told him so, one look at her would have confirmed it. A brief, intense affair would give pleasure to them both.

He would go about this differently, then. He would have her, but not just once and not in a grimy loft. Damian ran his hands through his hair, straightened his tie and then made his way briskly out to the street.

CHAPTER FOUR

LAUREL'S APARTMENT took up the second floor of a converted town house on the upper east side of Manhattan. The rooms were sun-filled and pleasant, and the building itself was handsome and well located.

But it was an old building, and sometimes the plumbing was a problem. The landlord kept promising repairs but the handful of tenants figured he was almost as ancient as the plumbing. None of them had the heart to keep after him, especially when it turned out that Grey Morgan, the hunky soap star in apartment 3G, had been a plumber's apprentice back in the days when he'd still been known as George Mogenovitch of Brooklyn.

His pretty dancer wife, Susie, had turned into a close friend, but she was another in what Laurel thought of as a legion of inveterate matchmakers. At least she had learned to read the signs. When Susie made spaghetti and invited her to supper, she accepted happily. When the invitation was for Beef Stroganoff and a good bottle of wine, it was wise to plead an excuse.

Laurel smiled to herself. Susie and George were the most warmhearted people imaginable, which explained why she was sitting on the closed lid of the toilet in her bathroom with a bunch of tools in her lap while George stood in her bathtub and tried to figure out why no water at all was coming out of the shower.

"Sorry it's taking me so long," he said, grunting as he worked a wrench around a fitting. "But I think I've almost got it."

"Hey," Laurel said, "don't apologize. I'm just grateful you're willing to bother."

George flicked back his blond mane and shot her a grin.

"Susie wouldn't have it any other way," he said. "She figures it keeps me humble."

Laurel smiled. "Clever Susie."

Not that George needed to be kept humble. He was a nice guy. Success hadn't gone to his head the way it did with some men. Hand them some good looks, some money, fame and fortune, and what did you get?

A man like Damian Skouras, that's what. Laurel's mouth thinned. Or like Kirk Soames. What was it about her that attracted such superficial, self-centered bastards?

Of course, she hadn't seen it that way, not at first. She was a woman accustomed to making her own way in the world; she'd learned early on that many men were threatened by her fame, her independence, even her beauty. So when Kirk—powerful, rich and handsome—came on to her with wry certainty and assurance, she'd found it intriguing. By the time he'd asked her to move in with him, she'd been head over heels in love.

Annie had told her, straight out, that she was making a mistake.

"Move in with him?" she'd said. "What ever happened to, 'Marry me?'"

"He's cautious," Laurel had replied, in her lover's defense, "and why wouldn't he be? Marriage is a tough deal for a man like that."

"It's a tough deal for anybody," Annie had said wryly. "Still, if he loves you and you love him..."

"Annie, I'm thirty-two. I'm old enough to live with a man without the world coming to an end. Besides, I don't want to rush into anything, any more than Kirk does."

"Uh-huh," Annie had said, in a way that made it clear she knew Laurel was lying. And she was. She'd have married Kirk in a second, if he'd asked. And he *would* ask, given time. She'd been certain of that.

"Laurel?"

Laurel blinked. George was looking at her, his brows

raised. "Hand me that other wrench, will you? The one with the black handle."

So she had moved in with Kirk, more or less, though she'd held on to her apartment. It had been his suggestion. He'd even offered to pay her rent, though she had refused. If she kept her apartment, he'd said, she'd have a place to stay when she had shoots or showings in the city because he lived thirty miles out, in a sprawling mansion on Long Island's North Shore.

"Bull," Annie had snorted. "The guy's a zillionaire. How come he doesn't have an apartment in the city?"

"Annie," Laurel had said patiently, "you don't understand. He needs the peace and quiet of the Long Island house."

In the end, it had turned out that he did have a Manhattan apartment. Laurel closed her eyes against the rush of painful memories. She'd learned about it by accident, fielding a phone call from a foolishly indiscreet building manager who'd wanted to check with Mr. Soames about a convenient time for some sort of repair to the terrace.

Puzzled, telling herself it was some sort of mistake or perhaps a surprise for her, Laurel had gone to the East side address and managed to slip inside when the doorman wasn't looking. She'd ridden the elevator to the twentieth floor, taken a deep breath and rung the bell of Apartment 2004.

Kirk had opened the door, dressed in a white terry-cloth robe. His face paled when he saw her but she had to give him credit; he recovered quickly.

"What are you doing here, Laurel?"

Before she could reply, a sultry voice called, "Kirk? Where are you, lover?" and a porcelain-skinned blonde wearing a matching robe and the flushed look that came of a long afternoon in bed, appeared behind him.

Laurel hadn't said a word. She hadn't even returned to the Long Island house for her things. And when the story got out, as it was bound to do, the people who knew her sighed and said well, it was sad but they'd have sworn Kirk had changed, that once he'd asked her to move into that big house on the water they'd all figured it meant he'd finally decided to settle down...

"You got a bad diverter valve," George muttered, "but I've almost got it under control. Takes time, that's all."

Laurel gave him an absent smile. Everything took time. It had taken her months to get over the pain of Kirk's betrayal but once she had, she'd begun thinking about their affair with the cold, clear logic of hindsight and she'd found herself wondering what she'd ever found attractive about a man like that to begin with.

She'd mistaken his arrogance for self-assurance, his egotism for determination. She, who'd always prided herself on her control, had been stupidly taken in by sexual chemistry, and the truth was that not even that had really lived up to its promise. She'd never felt swept away by passion in Kirk's arms.

But Damian's kiss had done that. It had filled her with fire, and with a longing so hot and sweet it had threatened to destroy her.

The tools Laurel was holding fell from her suddenly nerveless fingers and clattered on the tile floor.

"You okay?" George said, glancing over at her.

"Sure," she said quickly, and she bent down and scooped up the tools.

Damian Skouras was not for her. He was nothing but an updated copy of Kirk, right down to the sexy blonde pouting in the background at the wedding.

"Gimme the screwdriver, Laurel," George said. "No, not the Phillips head. The other one."

Had the man really thought she wouldn't notice the blonde? Or didn't he think it mattered?

"Egotistical bastard," she muttered, slapping the screwdriver into George's outstretched hand.

"Hey, what'd I do?"

Laurel blinked. George was looking at her as if she'd lost her mind.

"Oh," she said, and flushed bright pink. "George, I'm sorry. I didn't mean you."

He gave her the boyish grin that kept American women glued to their TV sets from two to three every weekday afternoon.

"Glad to hear it. From the look on your face, I'd hate to be whoever it is you're thinking about."

She'd never been able to bring herself to tell Annie the truth of her breakup with Kirk, not because Annie might have said, "I told you so," but because the pain had been too sharp.

"You were right" was all she'd told her sister, "Kirk wasn't for me."

Maybe I should have told her, Laurel thought grimly. Maybe, if I had, Annie and Dawn and everybody else at that wedding would have known Damian Skouras for the belly-to-the-ground snake he was.

"Got it," George said in triumph. He handed her the screwdriver and flipped the selector lever up and down. "Just you watch. Soon as I get out of the tub and turn this baby on—"

"Just be careful," Laurel said. "Watch out for that puddle of water in the..."

Too late. George yelped, lost his footing and made a grab for the first thing that was handy. It was the on-off knob. Water came pouring out of the shower head.

"Damn," he shouted, and leaped back, but it was too late. He was soaked, and so was Laurel. Half the icy spray had shot in her direction. Sputtering, George pushed the knob back in, shut off the water and flung his dripping hair back from his eyes. He looked down at himself, then eyed Laurel. "Well," he said wryly, "at least we know it works."

Laurel burst out laughing.

"Susie's going to think I tried to drown you," she said, tossing him a towel and dabbing at herself with another.

George yanked his soaked sweatshirt over his head and stepped out of the tub. His sneakers squished as he walked across the tile floor of the old-fashioned bathroom.

"I guess you'll have to phone old man Grissom," he said with a sheepish smile. "Tell him that valve's just about shot and he'd better send a plumber around to take a look."

"First thing in the morning," Laurel said, nodding. She mopped her face and hair, then hung the towel over the rack. "I'm just sorry you got drenched."

"No problem. Glad to help out." George draped his arm loosely around Laurel's shoulders. Together, they sauntered down the hall toward the front door. "As for the soaking— I was planning on entering a wet jeans contest anyway."

Laurel grinned, leaned back against the wall and crossed her arms.

"Uh-huh."

"Hey, they have wet T-shirt contests for women, right?" he said impishly as he reached for the doorknob. "Well, why not wet jeans contests for guys?" Grinning, he opened the door. "Anyhow, you know what they used to say. Save water, shower with a friend."

"Indeed," a voice said coldly.

Damian Skouras was standing in the doorway. He was dressed in a dark suit and a white shirt; his tie was a deep scarlet silk, and his face was twisted in a scowl.

Laurel's throat constricted. She'd been kidding herself. The man wasn't a copy of anybody, not when it came to looks. Kirk had been handsome but the only word that described Damian was the one she'd come up with this morning.

He was gorgeous.

He was also uninvited. And unwelcome. Definitely unwelcome, she reminded herself, and she stepped away from the wall, drew herself up to her full height and matched his scowl with one of her own.

"What," she asked coldly, "are you doing here?"

Damian ignored the question. He was too busy trying to figure out what in hell was going on.

What do you think is going on you idiot? he asked himself, and his frown deepened.

Laurel was wearing a soaked T-shirt that clung to her like a second skin. Beneath it, her rounded breasts and nipples stood out in exciting relief. She had on a pair of faded denim shorts, her feet were bare, her hair was wet and her face was shiny and free of makeup.

She was more beautiful than ever.

"Laurel? You know this guy?"

Damian turned his head and looked at the man standing beside her. Actually he wasn't standing beside her anymore. He'd moved slightly in front of her, in a defensive posture that made it clear he was ready to protect Laurel at all costs. Damian's lip curled. What would a woman see in a man like this? He was good-looking; women would think so, anyway, though he had too pretty a face for all the muscles that rippled in his bare chest and shoulders. Damian's gaze swept down the man's body. His jeans were tight and wet, and cupped him with revealing intimacy.

What the hell had been going on here? Laurel and the Bozo looked as if they'd just come in out of the rain.

Unfortunately, it hadn't rained in days.

He thought of what the guy had said about showering with a friend. It was, he knew, a joke. Besides, people didn't shower with their clothing on. Logic told him that, the same as it told him that they didn't climb out of bed wet from head to toe, but what the hell did logic have to do with anything?

Coming here, unannounced, had seemed such a clever idea. Catch her by surprise, have the limousine waiting downstairs with a chilled bottle of champagne in the built-in bar, long-stemmed roses in a crystal vase and reservations at that restaurant that had just opened with the incredible view of the city.

It hadn't occurred to him that just because the telephone directory listed an L. Bennett at this address was no guarantee that she lived alone.

"Laurel?"

The Bozo was talking to Laurel again but he hadn't taken his eyes off him.

"What's the deal? Do you know this guy?"

"Of course she knows me," Damian snapped.

"Is that right, Laurel?"

She nodded with obvious reluctance. "I know him. But I didn't invite him here."

The Bozo folded his arms over his chest. "She knows you," he said to Damian, "but she didn't invite you here."

"I don't know how to break this to you, mister...?"

"Morgan," George said. "Grey Morgan."

Damian smiled pleasantly. "I don't know how to break this to you, Mr. Morgan, but I understood every word she said."

"Then you'll be sure to understand this, too," Laurel said. "Go away."

"Go away," the Bozo repeated, and unfolded his arms.

His height, and all those rippling muscles, were impressive. Good, Damian thought. He could feel the same sense of anticipation spreading through his body again, the one he'd had this afternoon when he'd wanted nothing so much as to take that photographer apart.

Maybe he'd been sitting in too many boardrooms lately, exercising his mind instead of his muscles.

Laurel was thinking almost the same thing, though not in such flattering terms. What was with this man? She could almost smell the testosterone in the air. Damian's jaw was set, his eyes glittered.

George, his buffed torso and his tight jeans, was oozing muscle; Damian was the epitome of urbanity in his expensive dark suit...but she didn't for a second doubt which of them would win if it came down to basics.

Arrogant, self-centered, accustomed to having the world

dance to his tune, and now it looked as if he had all the primitive instincts of a cobra, she thought grimly. How in hell was she going to get rid of him?

"Laurel doesn't want you here, mister."

"What are you?" Damian said softly. "Her translator?"

"Listen here, pal, Laurel and I are—"

"We're very close," Laurel said. She moved forward, slipped her arm through the Bozo's, looked up and gave him a smile that sent Damian's self-control slipping another notch. "Aren't we, George—I mean, Grey?"

"Yeah," the Bozo said, after half a beat, "we are. Very, very close."

Damian's brows lifted. Maybe George or Grey or whoever he was, was right. Maybe he did need a translator. Something was going on here but he couldn't get a handle on it. He felt the way he sometimes did when he was doing business in Tokyo. Everyone spoke some English, Damian could manage some Japanese, but once in a while, a word or a phrase seemed to fall through the cracks.

"So if you don't mind, Mr. Skouras," Laurel said, putting heavy emphasis on the *mister*, "we'd appreciate it if you would—"

"George? Honey, are you done up there?"

They all looked down the hall. A pretty brunette stood at the bottom of the steps, smiling up at them.

"Hi, Laurel. Are you done borrowing my husband?"

Damian's brows arced again. He looked at Laurel, who flushed and dropped the Bozo's arm.

"Hi, Suze. Yeah, just about."

"Great." The brunette came trotting up the stairs. "Did he do a good job?"

Laurel's color deepened. "Fine," she said quickly.

"You see, George?" The brunette dimpled. "If the ratings ever go into the toilet, you can always go back to fixing them."

Laurel swallowed hard. Damian could see the movement of the muscles in her throat.

"He fixed my shower," she said, with dignity.

Damian nodded. "I see."

"Suze," George said, clearing his throat, "Laurel's got a bit of a problem here..."

"No," Laurel said quickly, "no, I don't."

"But you said...?"

"It's not a problem at all." She looked at Damian. "Mr. Skouras was just leaving. Weren't you, Mr. Skouras?"

"Yes, I was."

"You see? So there's no need to—"

"Just as soon as you change your clothing," he said. He leaned back against the door jamb, arms folded, and gave her a long, assessing look. "On the other hand, what you're wearing is...rather interesting. You might want to put on a pair of shoes, though. You never know what you're liable to step in, on a New York street."

He had to bite his lip to keep from laughing at the expression that swept over Laurel's face.

"I know what *you've* stepped in," she said, her chin lifting and her eyes blazing into his, "but I promise you, I've no intention of going anywhere with you."

"But our reservation is for eight," he said blandly.

A little furrow appeared between Laurel's eyebrows. "What reservation?"

"For dinner."

The furrow deepened. "Dinner?"

Damian looked at Susie. They shared a conspiratorial smile. "I'd be insulted that she forgot our appointment, but I know what a long day she put in doing that Redwood Computer layout."

"Redwood?" Susie said.

"Redwood?" George said, with interest, "the outfit that makes those hot portables?"

Damian shrugged modestly. "Well, that's what Wall Street says. I'm just pleased Laurel's doing the ads for the company." He smiled. "Almost as pleased as I am to have had the good fortune to have purchased Redwood."

"Redwood Comp...?" Susie's eyes widened. "Of course. Skouras. *Damian* Skouras. I should have recognized you. I was just reading *Manhattan Magazine*. Your picture's in it." A smile lit her pretty face. "George?" she said, elbowing her husband in the ribs, "this is..."

"Damian Skouras." George stuck out his hand, drew it back and wiped it on his damp jeans, then stuck it out again. "A pleasure, Mr. Skouras."

"Please, call me Damian," Damian said modestly.

George grinned as the men shook hands. "My wife and I just bought a hundred shares of your stock."

Damian smiled. "I'm delighted to hear it."

I don't believe this, Laurel thought incredulously. Was it a conspiracy? First Annie and Dawn, her very own flesh and blood; now Susie and George...

"Laurel," Susie said, "you never said a word!"

"About what?"

"About...about this," Susie said, with a little laugh.

"Suze, you've got this all wrong."

"You're not posing for those ads?"

"Yes. Yes, I am, but—but this man—"

"Damian," Damian said with a smile.

"This man," Laurel countered, "has nothing to do with—"

"My advertising people selected Laurel. With my approval, naturally."

"Naturally," Susie echoed.

"Imagine my surprise when we bumped into each other at my ward's wedding yesterday." His smile glittered. "In the flesh, as it were. We had a delightful few hours. Didn't we, Laurel? And we agreed to have dinner together tonight. To discuss business, of course."

Susie's eyes widened. She looked at Laurel, who was watching Damian as if she wished a hole in the ground would open under his feet.

"Of course," Susie said, chuckling.

"At *The Gotham Penthouse.*"

"The Gotham Penthouse! I just read a review of it in—"

"Manhattan Magazine?" Laurel said, through her teeth.

Susie nodded. "Uh-huh. It's supposed to be scrumptious!"

Damian smiled. "So I hear. Perhaps you and—is it George?"

"Yeah," George said. God, Laurel thought with disgust, it was a good thing there was no dirt on the floor or he'd have been scuffing his toes in it. "It is. Grey's my stage name. My agent figured it sounded better."

"Sexier," Susie said, and smiled up at her husband.

"Well, perhaps you and your wife would like to join us?"

"No," Laurel said sharply. Everyone looked at her. "I mean—I mean, of course, that would be lovely, but it isn't as if—"

"You don't have to explain." Susie looped her arm through her husband's. "It's a very romantic place, *The Penthouse*. Well, that's what the reviewer said, anyway."

Her smile was warm. It encompassed both Damian and Laurel as if they were a package deal. Laurel wanted to grab Susie and shake her until her teeth rattled. Or slug Damian Skouras in the jaw. Or maybe do both.

"You guys don't need an old married couple like us around."

"Susie," Laurel said grimly, "you really do not understand."

"Oh, I do." Susie grinned. "It's business. Right, Damian?"

Could a snake really smile? This one could.

"Precisely right," Damian said.

"It would be lovely to get together for dinner some other time, though. At our place, maybe. I do a mean Beef Stroganoff—which reminds me, George, if we don't get moving, everything will be burned to a crisp."

George's face suddenly took on a look of uncertainty. "Laurel? You're okay with this?"

A muscle worked in Laurel's jaw. At least somebody was still capable of thinking straight, but why drag innocent bystanders into the line of fire? This was a private war, between her and Damian.

"It's fine," she said. "And thanks for fixing the shower."

"Hey, anytime." George held out his hand, and Damian took it. "Nice to have met you."

"The same here," Damian said politely.

Susie leaned toward Laurel behind her husband's broad back.

"You never said a word," she announced in a stage whisper that could have been heard two floors below. "Laurel, honey, this guy is *gorgeous*!"

This guy's a rat, Laurel thought, but she bit her tongue and said nothing.

Susie had been right. The restaurant was a winner.

It had low lighting, carefully spaced tables and a magnificent view. The service was wonderful, the wine list impressive and the food looked delicious.

Laurel had yet to take a bite.

When she'd ignored the menu, Damian had simply ordered for them both. Beluga caviar, green salads, roast duck glazed with Montmorency cherries and brandy and, for a grand finale, a chocolate soufflé garnished with whipped cream that looked as light as air.

Neither the waiter nor Damian seemed to notice her hunger strike. The one served each course, then cleared it away; the other ate, commented favorably on the meal, and kept up a light, pleasant conversation in which she refused to join.

"Coffee?" Damian said, when the soufflé had been served. "Or do you prefer tea?"

Even prisoners on hunger strikes drank liquids. Laurel looked across the table at him.

"Which are you having?"

"Coffee. As strong as possible, and black."

Coffee was what she always drank, and just that way. Laurel gave a mental sigh.

"In that case," she said, unsmiling, "I'll have tea."

Damian laughed as the waiter hurried off. "Is there anything I could do to make you less inclined to insult me?"

"Would you do it, if there were?"

"Why do I have the feeling your answer might prove lethal?"

"At least you got *that* right!"

He sighed and shook his head, though she could see amusement glinting in his eyes. "That's not a very ladylike answer."

"Since you're obviously not a gentleman, why should it be? And I'm truly delighted to have provided you with a laugh a minute today. First Haskell, then George and Susie, and now here I am, playing jester for the king while he dines."

"Is that what you think?" Damian waited until their coffee and tea were served. "That I brought you here to amuse me?"

"I think you get your kicks out of tossing your weight around."

"Sorry?"

"You like to see people dance to your tune."

He pushed aside his dessert plate, moved his cup and saucer in front of him and folded his hands around the cup.

"That is not why I asked you to join me this evening."

"Asked? Coerced, you mean."

"I had every intention of asking you politely, Laurel, but when you opened the door and I saw you with that man, Grey…"

"His name is George."

"George, Grey, what does it matter?" Damian's eyes darkened. "I saw him, half-dressed. And I saw you smiling at him. And I thought, very well, I have a choice to make. I can do as I intended, ask her to put aside the words that passed between us this morning and come out to dinner with me..."

"The answer would have been no."

"Or," he said, his voice roughening, "I can punch this son of a bitch in the jaw, sling her over my shoulder and carry her off."

The air seemed to rush out of the space between them. Laurel felt as if she were fighting for breath.

"That—that's not the least bit amusing."

"It wasn't meant to be." Damian reached across the table and took her hand. "Something happened between us yesterday."

"I don't know what you're talk—"

"Don't!" His fingers almost crushed hers as she sought to tug free of his grasp. "Don't lie. Not to me. Not to yourself." A fierce, predatory light blazed in his eyes. "You know exactly what I'm talking about. I kissed you, and you kissed me back."

Their eyes met. He wasn't a fool; lying would get her nowhere. Well, her years before the camera had taught her some things, at least.

"So what?" she said coolly. She forced a faintly mocking smile to her lips. "You caught me off guard but then, you know that. What more do you want, Damian? My admission that you kiss well? I'm sure you know that, too—or doesn't your blond friend offer enough plaudits to satisfy that ego of yours?"

"Is that what this is all about? Gabriella?" Damian made an impatient gesture. "That's over with."

"She didn't like watching her lover flirt with another woman, you mean?" Laurel wrenched her hand free of his. "At least she's not a total idiot."

"I broke things off last evening."

"Last...? Not because of..."

"It was over between us weeks ago. I just hadn't gotten around to admitting it." A smile curled across his mouth. "It hadn't occurred to me that you'd be jealous."

"Jealous? Of you and that woman? Your ego isn't big, it's enormous! I don't even know you."

"Get to know me, then."

"There's no point. I'm not interested in getting involved."

"I'm not asking you to marry me," he said bluntly. "We're consenting adults, you and I. And something happened between us the minute we saw each other."

"Uh-huh. And next, you're going to tell me that nothing like this has ever happened to you before."

Laurel put her napkin on the table and slid to the end of the banquette. She'd listened to all she was going to listen to, and it wasn't even interesting. His line was no different than a thousand others.

"Laurel."

He caught her wrist as she started to rise. His eyes had gone black; the bones in his handsome, arrogant face stood out.

"Come to bed with me. Let me make love to you until neither of us can think straight."

Color flooded her face. "Let go," she said fiercely, but his hand only tightened on hers.

"I dreamed of you last night," he whispered. "I imagined kissing your soft mouth until it was swollen, caressing your breasts with my tongue until you sobbed with pleasure. I dreamed of being deep inside you, of hearing you cry out my name as you came against my mouth."

She wanted to flee his soft words but she couldn't, even if he had let her. Her legs were weak; she could feel her pulse pounding in her ears.

"That is what I've wanted, what we've both wanted, from the minute we saw each other. Why do you try to deny it?"

The bluntness of his words, the heat in his eyes, the memory of what she'd felt in his arms, stole her breath away and, with it, all her hard-won denial.

Everything Damian had said was true. She couldn't pretend anymore. She didn't like him. He was everything she despised and more, but she wanted him as she'd never wanted any man, and with such desperate longing that it terrified her.

Her vision blurred. She saw herself in his arms, lying beneath him and returning kiss for kiss, wrapping her legs around his waist as she tilted her hips up to meet his possessive thrusts.

"Yes," he said fiercely, and she looked into his eyes and knew that the time for pretense was over.

Laurel gave a soft cry. She tore her hand from Damian's, shot to her feet and flew from the restaurant, but he caught up to her just outside the door, his fingers curling around her arm like a band of steel.

"Tell me I'm wrong," he said in a hoarse whisper, "and so help me God, I'll have my driver take you home and you'll never be bothered by me again."

Time seemed to stand still. They stood in the warmth and darkness of the spring night, looking at each other, both of them breathing hard, and then Laurel whispered Damian's name and moved into his arms with a hunger she could no longer deny.

CHAPTER FIVE

THEY WERE INSIDE the limousine, shut off from the driver and the world, moving swiftly through the late-night streets of the city. The car, and Damian, were all that existed in Laurel's universe.

His body was rock-hard; his arms crushed her to him. His mouth was hot and open against hers, and his tongue penetrated her in an act of intimacy so intense it made her tremble. She felt fragile and feminine, consumed by his masculinity. His kiss demanded her complete surrender and promised, in return, the fulfilment of her wildest fantasies.

There would be no holding back. Not tonight. Not with him.

Wrong, this is wrong. Those were the words that whispered inside her head, but the message beating in her blood was far louder. *Stop thinking,* it said. *Let yourself feel.*

And she could feel. Everything. The hardness of Damian's body. The wildness of his kisses. The heat of his hands as he touched her. It was all so new... and yet, it wasn't. They had just met, but Damian was not a stranger. Was this why some people believed they'd lived before? She felt as if she'd known him in another life, or maybe since the start of time.

Her head fell back against his shoulder as his hand swept over her, skimming the planes of her face, stroking the length of her throat, then cupping her breast. His thumb brushed across her nipple and she cried out against his mouth.

He said her name in a husky whisper, and then something more, words in Greek that she couldn't understand. But she understood this, the way his fingertips trailed fire over her

65

skin, and this, the taste of his mouth, and yes, she understood when he clasped her hand and brought it to him so that she could feel the power and rigidity of his need.

"Yes," she said breathlessly, and he made a sound low in his throat, pushed up her skirt, slid his hand up her leg and cupped the molten heat he found between her thighs.

The shock of his touch, the raw sexuality of it, shot like lightning through Laurel's blood. A soft cry broke from her throat and she grabbed for his wrist. What she felt—what he was making her feel—was almost more than she could bear.

"Damian," she sobbed, "Damian, please."

"Tell me what you want," he said in a fierce whisper. "Say it."

You, she thought, I want you.

She did. Oh, she did. She wanted him in a way she'd never wanted any man, not just with her body but with something more, something she couldn't define...

The half-formed realization terrified her, and she twisted her face away from Damian's seeking mouth.

"Listen to me," she said urgently. Her fingers dug into his wrist. "I don't think—"

"Don't think," he said, "not tonight," and before she could respond, he thrust his hands into her hair, lifted her face to his and kissed her.

It was not the civilized thing to do.

Damian knew it, even as he took Laurel's mouth again.

The same wild need was beating in her blood as in his. He felt it in her every sigh, her caresses, her hungry response to his kisses. But she'd started to draw back, frightened, he suspected, of the passionate storm raging between them.

Hell, he couldn't blame her.

Something was happening here, something he didn't pretend to understand. The only thing he was sure of was that whatever this was, it was too powerful, too elemental, to deny. He'd sooner have given up breathing than give up this moment.

Minutes ago, when he'd touched her, when he'd felt the heat of her and she'd given that soft, keening cry of surrender, he'd damn near ripped off her panties, unzipped his fly and buried himself deep inside her.

That he hadn't done it had had little to do with propriety, or even with reason, though it would have been nice to tell himself so. The truth was simpler, and much more basic. What had stopped him was the burning need to undress her slowly, to savor her naked beauty with his eyes and hands and mouth.

He wanted to watch her face as he slowly caressed her, to see her pupils grow enormous with pleasure, to touch her and stroke her until she was wild for his possession. He wanted her in bed, his bed, naked in his arms, her skin hot against his, climbing toward a climax that would be more powerful than anything either of them had ever known, and though the intensity of his need was setting off warning bells, he didn't give a damn. Not now. His body was hot and hard; he wanted Laurel more than he'd ever wanted anything, or anyone, in this world.

She'd told him, in the restaurant, that he wasn't a gentleman but hell, he'd never been a gentleman, not from the moment of his birth. Now, as he cupped her face in his hands and whispered her name, as her eyes opened and met his, he knew that he'd sooner face the fires of hell than start pretending to be a gentleman tonight.

He lived in an apartment on Park Avenue.

It was a penthouse duplex, reached by a private elevator that opened onto a dimly lighted foyer that rose two stories into darkness. If he had servants, they were not visible.

The elevator doors slid shut, and they were alone.

Shadows, black-velvet soft and deep, wrapped around them. The night was so still that Laurel could hear the pounding beat of her heart.

There was still time. She could say, "This was a mistake," and demand to be taken home. Damian wouldn't like it, but what did that matter? She was neither a fool nor a tramp, and surely only a woman who was one or both would be on her way to bed with a man she'd met little more than twenty-four hours ago.

Damian's hands closed on her shoulders. He turned her toward him, and what she saw mirrored in his eyes drove every logical thought from her mind.

"Laurel," he said, and she went into his arms.

He kissed her hard, lifting her against him, his hands cupping her bottom so that she was pressed against his erection. His mouth teased hers open. He bit down on her bottom lip, then soothed the tiny wound with his tongue, until she was trembling and clutching his jacket for support.

"Say it now," he said in a savage whisper. "Tell me what you want."

The answer was in her eyes, but she gave it voice.

"You," she said in a broken whisper, "you, you—"

Damian's mouth dropped to hers. Heart surging with triumph, he lifted her into his arms and carried her up the stairs, into the darkness.

His bedroom was huge. The bed, bathed in ivory moonlight, faced onto a wall of glass below which the city glittered in the night like a castle from a fairy tale.

Slowly Damian lowered Laurel to her feet. For a long moment, he didn't touch her. Then he lifted his hand and stroked her cheek. Laurel closed her eyes and leaned into his caress.

Gently he ran his hand over her hair.

"Take it down," he said softly.

Her eyes flew open. She couldn't see his face clearly— he was standing in shadow—but there was an intensity in the way he held himself.

"My hair?" she whispered.

"Yes." He reached out and touched the silky curls that lay against her neck. "Take it down for me."

Laurel raised her hands to the back of her head. Her hair had already started coming loose of the tortoiseshell pins she'd used to put it up. Now, she removed the pins slowly, wishing she could see his face as she did. But he was still standing in shadow, and he didn't step forward until her hair tumbled around her shoulders.

"Beautiful," he whispered.

He caught a fistful of the shining auburn locks and brought them to his lips. Her hair felt like silk against his mouth and its fragrance reminded him of a garden after a gentle spring rain.

He let her hair drift from his fingers.

"Now your earrings," he said softly.

Her hands went to the tiny crystal beads that swayed on slender gold wires from her earlobes. He could see confusion in her eyes and he knew she'd expected something different, a quicker leap into the flames, but if that was what she wanted, he wouldn't, hell, he *couldn't*, oblige. His control was stretched almost to the breaking point. He couldn't touch her now; if he did, it would all be over before it began, and he didn't want that.

Nothing would be rushed. Not with her. Not tonight.

One earring, then the other, dropped into her palm. Damian held out his hand, and she gave them to him. Her hands went to the silver buttons on her silk jacket, and he nodded. Seconds later, the jacket fell to the floor.

He reached out and caught her wrists.

"Nothing more," he whispered, and brushed his mouth over hers. "I want to do all the rest."

She heard the soft urgency in his voice, the faint tone of command. His eyes glittered; there was a dark passion in his face, a taut pull of skin over bone that made her heart beat faster.

But his touch was gentle as he undressed her. And he did it slowly, so slowly that she thought she might die with the pleasure of it, first her blouse, then her skirt, her slip and her bra, until she stood before him wearing nothing but her high-heeled sandals, sheer stockings, a garter belt and panties that were a lacy wisp of white silk.

She heard his breath hitch in his throat. He stepped back and looked at her. She felt a flush rise over her skin and she started to cross her arms over her breasts, but he stopped her.

"Don't hide yourself from me," he said thickly. "Laurel, *mátya mou*, how exquisite you are."

She wanted to ask him what it meant, the name he'd called her; she wanted to tell him that no matter what he thought, this night was a first for her, that she'd never given herself to anyone this way, never wanted anyone this way.

There were a hundred things to say, but she couldn't bring herself to say anything but his name.

"Yes," he said, and he lifted her in his arms again, kissed her deeply and carried her to the bed.

He undid the garters, rolled down her stockings and dropped them to the floor. He lifted each of her feet and kissed the high, elegant arches; he sucked her toes into his mouth. Then he knelt beside her and undid the tiny hooks on the garter belt. His hands shook as he did, which was strange because while he'd never counted them, he'd surely undone a thousand such closures before. He had done all these things before, taken a woman to his bed, undressed her...and yet, when Laurel finally lay naked before him, he felt his heart kick against his ribs.

He whispered her name and then he put one arm beneath her shoulders and lifted her to him, kissed her mouth as she curled her hands into the folds of his jacket. There was a tightness growing deep within him, one that threatened to shatter what little remained of his control. He knew it was time to stop touching her. He needed to rip off his clothing and bury himself inside her or risk humiliating himself like an untried boy, but he couldn't.

Nothing could keep him from learning the taste and feel of her skin.

He kissed her breasts, drawing the beaded nipples deep into his mouth, and when she cried out his name and arced toward him, her excitement fueled his own. He ran his hand along her hip, his fingers barely stroking across the feathery curls that formed a sweet, inverted triangle between her thighs, and the tightness in his belly grew.

"Laurel," he said. "Look at me."

Her lashes fluttered open. Her eyes were huge, the blue irises all but consumed by the black pupils. She was breathing hard; her face, her rounded breasts, were stained with the crimson flush of passion.

He had done this to her, he thought fiercely, he had brought her this pleasure. He said her name again, his gaze holding hers as he moved his hand lower and when, at last, he touched her, she let out a cry so soft and wild that he thought he could feel it against his palm.

He rolled away from her and stripped off his clothing. His hands shook; it was as if he was entering into an unknown world where what awaited him could bring joy beyond imagining or the darkness of despair. He didn't know which right know, and he didn't give a damn.

All that mattered was this moment, and this woman.

Laurel. Beautiful Laurel.

Naked, he knelt on the bed beside her. She was watching him, her face pale but for the glow on her cheeks, and the urgency deep within him seemed to diminish. Just for a moment, he thought it might almost be enough to take her in his arms, kiss her, hold her close and listen to the beat of her heart against his the whole night through.

But then she whispered his name and held her arms up to him, and he knew that he needed more. He needed to penetrate her, to make her his in the way men have done since the dawn of time.

"Laurel," he said, and when her eyes met his, he gave up thinking, parted her thighs and sank deep into her heat.

* * *

Laurel rose carefully from the bed.

It was very late, and Damian was asleep. She was sure of it; she could hear the steady susurration of his breath.

Her clothing was scattered across the room. She gathered up the bits and pieces, moving quietly so as not to wake him, and she thought about how he had undressed her, how she'd let him undress her, how she'd wanted him to undress her.

A hot, sick feeling roiled in the pit of her stomach.

The apartment was silent as she slipped out of his bedroom, though the darkness had given way to a cheerless grey. It made it easier to see, at least; the last thing she wanted to do was put on a light and risk waking him.

What in heaven's name had she done?

Sex, she told herself coldly. An experience, a seduction, the kind other women whispered about, even joked about. That was what had happened to her, a mind-blowing night of passion in the arms of a man who obviously knew his way around the boudoir.

Laurel's hands trembled as she zipped up her skirt.

She had given up all the moral precepts she'd lived by. She'd humiliated herself. She'd…she'd…

A moan broke from her throat. She'd become someone else, that was what had happened, and the knowledge that such a woman even existed inside her would haunt her forever.

The things she'd done tonight, the things she'd let Damian do…

What had happened to her? Just the sight of him, kneeling between her thighs, had made her come apart. He was so magnificent, such a perfect male animal, his broad shoulders gleaming as if they'd been oiled, his hair dark and tumbling around his face. The tiny gold stud, glinting in his ear, had been all the adornment such a man would ever need.

And then he'd entered her. She'd felt her body stretching to welcome him, to contain him…and then he'd moved, and moved again, and a cry had burst from her throat and she'd shattered into a million shining pieces.

"Damian," she'd sobbed, "oh, Damian..."

"I know," he'd whispered, his mouth on hers, and then she'd felt him beginning to move again, and she'd realized he was still hard within her. The flames had ignited more slowly the second time, not because she'd wanted him less but because he'd made it happen that way, pulling back, then easing forward, filling her and filling her, taking her closer and closer to the edge until, once again, she'd felt herself soar into the night sky where she'd blazed as brightly as a comet before tumbling back to earth.

She'd found paradise, she'd thought dreamily, as Damian's arms closed around her. She'd blushed as he whispered soft words to her and when, at last, he'd kissed her forehead, and her mouth, and held her close against his heart, she'd drifted into dreamless sleep.

Hours later, something—a sound, a whisper of breeze from the window—had awakened her. For a moment, she'd been confused. This wasn't her bedroom...

And then she'd remembered. She was in Damian's arms, in his bed, with the scent of him and what they'd done on her skin, and suddenly, in the cold, sharp light of dawn, she'd seen the night for what it really had been.

Cheap. Tawdry. Ugly.

Paradise? Laurel's throat constricted. A one-night stand, was more like it. She'd gone to bed with a stranger, not just gone to bed with him but—but done things with him she'd never...

...*felt things she'd never*...

"Laurel?"

She gasped and spun around. The bedroom door had opened; Damian stood in a pool of golden light that spilled from a bedside lamp. Naked, unashamed, he was a Greek statue come to life, hewn not of cold marble but of warm flesh. There was a little smile on his lips, a sexy, sleepy one, but as he looked at her, it began to fade.

"You're all dressed."

"Yes." Laurel cleared her throat. "I—I'm sorry if I woke you, Damian. I tried to be quiet but—"

God, she was babbling! She'd never sneaked out of a man's apartment before, but she'd be damned if she'd let him know that. Anyway, there was a first time for everything. Hadn't she proved that tonight?

"I apologize if I disturbed you."

"Apologize?" he said, his eyes narrowing.

"Yes. Oh, and thank you for..." *For what? Are you crazy? What are you thanking him for?* "For everything," she said brightly.

"Laurel..."

"No, really, you needn't see me out. I'm sure I can find my way, just down the stairs and through the—"

"Dammit," he said sharply, "what is this?"

"What is what? It's late. Very late. Or early, I don't really know which. And I have to go home, and change, and—" The quick, brittle flow of words ended in a gasp as he reached out and brought her against him. "Damian, don't."

"Ah," he said softly, "I understand." He laughed softly, bent his head and took the tip of her earlobe gently between his teeth. "Morning-after jitters. Well, I know how to fix that."

"Don't," she said again. She could hear the faint rasp in her own voice; it said, more clearly than words, that though her head meant one thing, her traitorous body meant something very different. She could feel him stirring against her and a warm heaviness settled in her loins.

"Laurel." Damian spoke in a whisper. He wasn't laughing now; he was looking at her through eyes that had darkened to silvery ash. "Come back to bed."

"No," she said, "I just told you, I can't."

His smile was honeyed. Slowly he dipped his head and kissed her, parting her lips with his.

"You can. And you want to. You know that you do."

She closed her eyes as he kissed the hollow of her throat. He was right, that was the worst of it. She wanted to go with him into that wide bed, where the scent of their love-making still lingered.

Except that it hadn't been lovemaking. It had been... There was a word for what they'd done, a word so ugly, so alien, that even thinking it made her feel unclean.

His hands were at the top button of her blouse. In a moment, he'd have them all undone, and then he'd touch her, and she wouldn't want to stop him...

"Stop it!" Her hands wrapped around his wrists. His brows, as black as a crow's wings, drew together. She'd taken him by surprise, she saw, and she made the most of the advantage and pressed on. "We had—we had fun, I agree, but let's not spoil it. Really, we both knew it was just one of those things that happen. There's no need to say anything more."

His eyes narrowed. "I thought we might—"

"Might what? Work out an arrangement?" She forced a smile to her lips. "I'm sorry, Damian, but I'd rather leave it at this. You know what they say about too much of any-thing spoiling it."

He was angry, she could see that in the flush that swept over his high cheekbones. His ego had taken a hit but that was too damn bad. What had he expected? An if-it's-Tuesday-it-must-be-your-place kind of deal, the sort he'd no doubt had with the blonde?

She waited, not daring to move, knowing that if he took her in his arms and kissed her again, her pathetic show of bravado might collapse—but he didn't. He studied her in silence, a muscle bunching in his cheek, and then he gave a curt nod.

"As you wish, of course. Actually you're quite right. Too much of anything is never good." He smiled politely, though she suspected the effort cost him, and turned toward the bedroom. "Just give me a minute to dress and I'll see you home."

"No! No, I'll take a taxi."

Damian swung toward her. "Don't be ridiculous."

"I'm perfectly capable of seeing myself home."

"Perhaps." His voice had taken on a flinty edge, as had his gaze. He folded his arms over his chest and she thought, fleetingly, that even in the splendor of his nudity, he managed to look imposing. "But this is New York City, not some little town in Connecticut, and I am not a man to permit a woman to travel these streets, alone, at this hour."

"Permit? *Permit*?" Laurel drew herself up. "I don't need your permission."

"Hell," he muttered, and thrust a hand into his hair. "This is nothing to quarrel about."

"You're right, it isn't. Goodbye, Damian."

His hand fell on her shoulder as she spun away from him, his fingers biting harshly into her flesh.

"What's going on here, Laurel? Can you manage to tell me that?"

"I have told you. I said—"

"I heard what you said, and I don't believe you." His touch gentled; she felt the rough brush of his fingertips against her throat. "You know you want more than this."

"You've no idea what I want," she said sharply.

He smiled. "Tell me, then. Let me get dressed, we'll have coffee and we'll talk."

"How many times do I have to say I'm not interested before you believe me, Damian?"

His eyes darkened. Long seconds passed, and then his hand fell from her shoulder. He turned, strode into his bedroom, picked up the telephone and punched a button on the dial.

"Stevens? Miss Bennett is leaving. Bring the car around, please."

"Why did you do that? There was no need to wake your chauffeur!"

He looked at her, his lips curved in a parody of a smile as he hung up the phone.

"I'm sure Stevens would appreciate your thoughtfulness, but he's been with me for years. He's quite accustomed to being awakened to perform such errands. Can you find your own way to the lobby, or shall I ring for the doorman?"

"I'll find my own way," she said quickly.

"Fine. In that case, if you'll excuse me…?"

The door shut gently in her face.

She stood staring at it, feeling a rush of crimson flood her skin, hating herself and hating him, and then she spun away.

Would she ever forget the stupidity of what she'd done tonight? she wondered, as she rode to the lobby in his private elevator.

More to the point, would she ever forget that the only place she'd ever glimpsed heaven had been in Damian Skouras's arms?

In the foyer of the penthouse, Damian stood at the closed doors to the elevator, glaring at the tiny lights on the wall panel as they marked Laurel's passage to the lobby. He'd put on a pair of jeans and zipped them, but he hadn't bothered closing them and they hung low on his hips.

What the hell had happened, between the last time they'd made love and now? He'd fallen asleep holding a warm, satisfied woman in his arms and awakened to find a cold stranger getting dressed in the hallway.

No, not a stranger. Laurel had metamorphosed back into who she'd been when they'd met, a beautiful woman with a tongue like a razor and the disposition of a grizzly bear. And she'd done her damnedest to make it sound as if what had gone on between them tonight had no more importance than a one-night stand.

The light on the panel blinked out. She'd reached the lobby, and the doorman, alerted by the call Damian had made after he'd closed the bedroom door, would be waiting to hand her safely off to Stevens.

Still glowering, he made his way to the terrace in time

to see Laurel getting into the car. Stevens shut the door after her, climbed behind the wheel and that was that.

She was gone, and good riddance.

Who was he kidding? She wasn't gone, not that easily. Her fragrance still lingered on his skin, and in his bed. The sound of her voice, the way she'd sighed his name while they were making love, drifted like a half-remembered tune in his mind.

He had lied to her, when he'd said Stevens was accustomed to being roused at all hours of the night. Being at the beck-and-call of an employer was something he'd hated, in his youth; he'd vowed never to behave so imperiously with those who served him.

Besides, waking Stevens had never been necessary before.

No woman had ever risen and left his bed so eagerly, Damian thought grimly, as he strode into his bedroom. His problem was usually getting rid of them, not convincing them to stay.

Not that he really cared. It had been pleasant, this interlude; he'd have been happy to have gone on with it for a few more weeks, even for a couple of months, but there were other women. There were always other women.

Something glittered on the carpet. Damian frowned and scooped it up.

It was Laurel's earring.

His hand closed hard around it. He remembered the flushed, expectant look on her face when he'd taken the earrings from her, when he'd begun undressing her, when she'd raised her arms to him and he'd knelt between her thighs and thrust home...

"Home?" he said. He laughed, then tossed the earring onto the night table.

It was late, he was tired, and when you came right down to it, the only thing special about tonight had been the sheer effort it had taken to get Laurel Bennett into his bed.

Whistling, Damian headed for the shower.

CHAPTER SIX

SUSIE MORGAN sat at Laurel's kitchen table, her chin propped on her fist as she watched Laurel knead a lump of sourdough batter.

Actually, Susie thought with a lifted eyebrow, Laurel was closer to beating the life out of the stuff than she was to kneading it. Susie glanced at her watch and her brow rose another notch. Laurel had been at it for fifteen minutes, well, fifteen minutes that she knew of, anyway. Who knew how long that poor mound of dough had really been lying there? When she'd come by for Laurel's if-I'm-home-and-haven't-gained-any-weight-the-camera-might-notice Friday morning bread-baking session, there'd already been a dab of flour on Laurel's nose and a mean glint in her eye.

The flour was one thing, but the glint was another. Susie frowned as Laurel whipped the dough over and punched it hard enough to make her wince in sympathy. She'd never known her friend to look so angry, not in the three years they'd known each other, but that was the way she looked lately...though there were times when another expression chased across her face, one that hinted not so much of anger but of terrible unhappiness.

Laurel had alternated between those two looks for four weeks now, ever since the night she'd gone out with Damian Skouras, whose name she hadn't once mentioned since. He hadn't come by again, either, which didn't make sense. Susie had seen the way he'd looked at Laurel and, whether Laurel knew it or not, the way she'd looked at him. Any self-respecting scientist caught between the two of them would have had doubts about carbon emissions being the only thing heating up the atmosphere.

Susie had given it another try, just the other day.

"How's Adonis?" she'd said, trying to sound casual.

Laurel had tried to sound casual, too. "Who?"

"The Greek," Susie had replied, playing along, "you know, the one with the looks and the money."

"How should I know?"

"Aren't you seeing him anymore?"

"I saw him once, under protest."

"Yeah, but I figured—"

"You figured wrong," Laurel had answered, in a way that made it clear the topic was off limits.

"Well, if you say so," Susie had said, "but, you know, if anything's on your mind and you want to talk about it…"

"Thanks, but there's nothing worth talking about," Laurel had replied with a breezy smile, which, as Susie had tried to tell George that night, was definitely proof that there was.

"I don't follow you," George had said patiently. So she'd tried to explain but George, sweet as he was, was a man. It was too much to expect he'd see that if there truly was nothing worth talking about, Laurel would have said something like, "What *are* you talking about, Susie?" instead of just tossing off that meaningless response. She'd even tried to explain that she had this feeling, just a hunch, really, that something had happened between Laurel and the Skouras guy, but George's eyes had only glazed over while he said, "Really?" and "You don't say," until finally she'd given it up.

Susie's frown deepened. On the other hand, even George might sense there was a problem if he could see Laurel beating the life out of that poor sourdough. A couple of more belts like the last and the stuff would be too intimidated to rise.

Susie cleared her throat.

"Uh, Laurel?"

"Yeah?"

"Ah, don't you think that's about done?"

Laurel gave the dough a vicious punch and blew a curl off her forehead.

"Don't I think what's about done?"

"The bread," Susie said, wincing as Laurel slammed her fist into the yeasty mound again.

"Soon." She gave the stuff another whack that made the counter shudder. "But not just yet."

Susie's mouth twitched. She sat up straight, crossed her long, dancer's legs and linked her hands around her knee.

"Anybody I know?" she said casually.

"Huh?"

"Whoever it is you're beating to death this morning. I figure there's got to be a face in that flour that only you can see."

Laurel ran the back of her wrist across her forehead.

"Your imagination's working overtime. I'm making bread, not working out my frustrations."

"Ah," Susie said knowingly. She watched Laurel give the dough a few more turns and punches before dumping it into a bowl and covering it with a damp dish towel. "Because," she said, going with instinct, "it occurred to me, it might just be Damian Skouras you were punching out."

Laurel turned away and tore a piece of paper towel from the roll above the sink. She thought of saying, "Why would you think that?" and looking puzzled, but she'd barely gotten away clean the last time Susie had raised Damian's name. Susie knew her too well, that was the problem.

"I told you," she said flatly, "I'm making bread."

"That's it?"

"That's it."

Susie cleared her throat again. "So, have you heard from him?"

"Suze, you asked me that just the other day. And I said that I hadn't."

"And that you don't expect to. Or want to."

"Right again." Laurel took the coffeepot from the stove

and refilled Susie's cup. She started to refill hers, too, but when she saw the glint of oil that floated on what remained, her stomach gave a delicate lurch. Wonderful. She had definitely picked up some sort of bug. Just what she needed, she thought, as she hitched her hip onto a stool opposite Susie's. "So, where's that handsome hunk of yours this morning?"

"At the gym, toning up his abs so he can keep his devoted fans drooling. And don't try to change the subject. It's *your* handsome hunk we were talking about."

"My...?" Laurel rolled her eyes. "What does it take to convince you? Damian Skouras isn't 'my' anything. Don't you ever give up?"

"No," Susie said, with disarming honesty. She lifted her cup with both hands, blew on the coffee, then took a sip. "Not when something doesn't make any sense. You are the most logical, levelheaded female I've ever known."

"Thank you, I think."

"Which is the reason I keep saying to myself, how could a logical, levelheaded female turn her back on a zillionaire Apollo?"

"It was 'Adonis' the last time around," Laurel said coolly. "Although, as far as I'm concerned, it doesn't matter what you call him."

"You didn't like him?"

"Susie, for heaven's sake..."

"Okay, okay, maybe I'm nuts—"

"There's no 'maybe' about it."

"But I just don't understand."

"That's because there isn't anything *to* understand. I keep telling you that. Damian Skouras and I went to dinner and—"

"Do you know, you do that whenever you talk about him?"

Laurel sighed, shook her head and gazed up at the ceiling. "Do what?"

"Well, first you call him DamianSkouras. One word, no pause, as if you hardly know the guy."

As if I hadn't slept with him, Laurel thought, and she felt a blaze of color flood her cheeks.

"Aha," Susie said, in triumph. "You see?"

"See what?"

"The blush, that's what. And the look that goes with it. They always follow, right on the heels of DamianSkouras."

Laurel rose, went to the sink and turned on the water. "I love you dearly, Suze," she said, squeezing in a shot of Joy, "but you are the nosiest thing going, did you know that?"

"George says I am, but what does he know?" Susie smiled. "Men don't understand that women love to talk about stuff like this."

"Stuff like what? There's nothing to talk about."

"There must be, otherwise you wouldn't turn into a clam each time I mention Damian's name."

"I do not turn into a clam. There just isn't anything to say, that's all."

"Listen, my friend, I was here that night, remember? I saw the way you guys looked at each other. And then, that was it. No further contact, according to you."

"Hand me that spoon, would you?"

"You can't blame me for wondering. The guy's gorgeous, he's a zillionaire and he's charming."

"Charming?" Laurel spun around, her cheeks flushed. "He's a scoundrel, that's what he is!"

"Why?"

"Because—because..." Laurel frowned. It was a good question. Damian hadn't seduced and abandoned her. What had happened that night hadn't been a Victorian melodrama. She'd gone to his bed willingly and left it willingly. If the memory haunted her, humiliated her, she had no one to blame but herself. "Susie, do me a favor and let's drop this, okay?"

"If that's the way you want it..."

"I do."

"Okay, then. Consider the subject closed."

"Great. Thank you."

"It's just that I'm really puzzled," Susie said, after a moment's silence. Laurel groaned, but Susie ignored her. "I mean, he looked at you the way a starving man would look at a seven-course meal. Why, if Ben Franklin had come trotting through this place that night, he wouldn't have needed a kite and a key to discover that lightning bolts and electricity are the same thing!"

"That's good, Suze. Keep going like that, you can give up dancing and start writing scripts for George's soap."

"You make it sound as if you didn't like him."

"You clever soul." Laurel flashed a saccharine smile. "How'd you ever come up with an idea like that?"

"Yeah, well, I don't believe you."

"You don't believe me? What's that supposed to mean?"

Susie rose, went to the pantry cabinet and opened it. "It means," she said, taking out a box of Mallomars, "that lightning must have struck somewhere because I've never known you to come traipsing in at dawn." She peered into the box. "Goody. Two left. One for you, and one for me."

Laurel glanced at the chocolate-covered marshmallow cookie Susie held out to her. Her stomach lifted again, did a quick two-step, then settled in place.

"I'll pass."

"I can have both?"

"Consider this your lucky day. And how do you know what time I came in?"

Susie bit into a cookie. "I went running that morning," she said around a mouthful of crumbs, "so I was up at the crack of dawn. You know me. I like the streets to myself. Besides, these old floors squeak like crazy. I could hear you marching around up here. Pacing, it sounded like, for what seemed like forever."

Not forever. Just long enough to try to believe there was

no point in hating myself for what I'd done because it was already part of the past and I'd never, not in a million years, do anything like it again.

"Where'd he take you that night, anyway?"

"You know where he took me." Laurel plucked a cup from the suds and scrubbed at it as if it were a burned roasting pan. "To dinner."

"And?" Susie batted her lashes. "Where else, hmm?"

To paradise in his arms, Laurel thought suddenly, and the feeling she'd worked so hard to suppress, the memory of how it had been that night, almost overwhelmed her.

Maybe she'd been a fool to leave him. Maybe she should have stayed. Maybe she should have taken up where the blonde had left off...

The cup slipped from her hands and smashed against the floor.

"Dammit," she said fiercely. Angry tears rose in her eyes and she squatted and began picking up the pieces of broken china. "You want to know what happened that night?" She stood up, dumped the pieces in the garbage and wiped her hands on the seat of her jeans. "Okay, I'll tell you."

"Laurel, honey, I didn't mean—"

"I slept with Damian Skouras."

Susie took a deep breath. "Wow."

"I slept with a guy I didn't know all that well, didn't like all that much and didn't ever want to see again, because—because—"

"I understand the because," Susie said softly.

Laurel spun toward her, her eyes glittering. "Don't patronize me, dammit! If *I* don't understand, how can you?"

"Because I slept with George, the first time we went out. That's how."

Laurel sank down on the edge of a stool. "You did?"

"I did. And I'd never done anything like it before."

"Well, then, why did you, that time?"

Susie smiled. "Who knows? Hormones? Destiny? It happened, that's all."

Laurel's smile was wobbly. "See? I was right, you ought to be writing for the soaps."

"Mostly, though, I did it because my body and my heart knew what my brain hadn't yet figured out. George and I were soul mates."

"Yeah, well, I don't have any such excuse. Damian Skouras and I are definitely not soul mates. I did what I did, and now I have to live with it."

"The bastard!"

Laurel laughed. "A minute ago, he was Adonis. Or was it Apollo?"

"A minute ago, I didn't know he'd taken advantage of you and then done the male thing."

"Trust me, Suze," Laurel said wryly, "he didn't take advantage of me. I was willing."

Susie plucked the remaining Mallomar from the box. "That's beside the point. He did the male thing, anyway. 'Wham, bam, thank you, ma'am—and maybe I'll call you sometime.'"

Laurel stared at her friend. Then she rose, yanked a piece of paper towel from the roll, dampened it in the sink and began to rub briskly at the countertop.

"I told him not to call."

"What?"

"You heard me. He wanted to see me again. I told him it was out of the question, that I wasn't interested in that kind of relationship."

"You and Damian made love, it was great and you told him you never wanted to see him again?"

"I didn't say that."

"That it wasn't great? Or that you never wanted to see him again?"

Laurel stared at Susie, and then she dropped her gaze and turned to the sink.

"What's your point?" she said, plunging her hands into the water.

"It's *your* point I'm trying to figure out here, my friend. Why did you make love with the guy and then tell him to hit the road?"

"I didn't 'make love' with him," Laurel said sharply. "I slept with him."

"Semantics," Susie said with a shrug.

"No, it's more than that. Look, Susie, what you did with George was different. You loved him."

"Still do," Susie said, with a little smile.

"Well, I didn't love Damian. I can't imagine loving Damian. He's such an arrogant, egotistical, super-macho SOB..."

"Sigh," Susie said, rolling her eyes.

Laurel laughed. "The point is, he's not my type."

"Nobody's your type. Name one guy since that bastard, Kirk Soames, who you've given more than a quick hello and I'll eat whatever it is you think you're gonna make out of that poor overbeaten, overkneaded, overpounded sourdough."

"And I'm not his type," Laurel finished, refusing to rise to the bait. She shut off the water, dried her hands on a dish towel and turned around. "That's the sum, total and end of it, so—so..."

Susie had just taken a bite of the Mallomar. A smear of dark chocolate and marshmallow festooned her upper lip.

"You only think so, babe. I saw the way you guys looked at each other."

Laurel swallowed hard. "There's a—a smudge of chocolate on your mouth, Suze."

"Yeah?" Susie scrubbed a finger over her lip. "Did I get it?"

"Most of it. There's still a little bit..." Laurel's stomach rose slowly into her throat. "That's it," she said weakly. "You've got it now." She turned away and wrapped her hands around the rim of the sink, waiting until her stomach settled back where it belonged.

"Laurel? You all right?"

Laurel nodded. "Sure. I'm just—"

"Tired of me poking my nose where it doesn't belong," Susie said. She sighed. "Listen, let's drop the subject. You want to talk about it, I'm here. You don't...?" She gave an elaborate shrug. "Tell you what. How about having supper with us tonight? George is making *pirogi*. Remember his *pirogi*? You loved 'em, the last time."

"Yes, I did. They were—they were..."

Laurel thought of the little doughy envelopes filled with onion-studded ground beef. She *had* loved them, it was true, but now all she could think about was how they'd glistened with butter, how the butter had slid down her throat like oil...

"They were delicious," she said brightly, "but—but this bread is my last extravagance for a while. I'm going on a quick diet. You know how it is. I've got a layout coming up and I need to drop a couple of pounds. Give me a rain check, okay?"

Susie leaned back against the counter. "Well, have supper with us anyway." She patted her belly. "It wouldn't hurt me to lose some weight, and you know those close-ups they give George. Forget the *pirogi*. We'll go wild, take out a couple of Lean Cuisine Veggie Lasagnas and zap 'em in the microwave. How's that sound?"

Lasagna. Laurel imagined bright red tomato sauce, smelled its acidic aroma. Saliva filled her mouth, and she swallowed hard.

"Actually, I may just pass on supper altogether. I think I've got some kind of bug. I did a shoot in Bryant Park last week. Everybody was coughing and sneezing like crazy, and I've felt rotten ever since."

"Summer colds," Susie said philosophically, as she popped what remained of the Mallomar into her mouth.

"The worst kind to shake. A couple of aspirin and some hot chicken soup ought to…Laurel? What's the matter?"

A bead of jelly, glistening like blood at the corner of Susie's mouth, that was what was the matter.

Laurel's belly clenched.

"Nothing," she said, "noth—" *Oh hell.* Her eyes widened and she groaned, clamped her hand over her mouth and shot from the room.

When she emerged from the bathroom minutes later, pale and shaken, Susie was waiting in the bedroom, sitting cross-legged in the middle of Laurel's bed, a worried look on her face.

"Are you okay?"

"I'm fine," Laurel said with a shaky smile.

"Fine, my foot." Susie looked at her friend's face. Laurel's skin was waxen, her eyes were glassy and her forehead glistened with sweat. "You're sick."

"I told you, Suze, it's just some bug I picked up."

"The one that had everybody on that photo session coughing and sneezing?"

"Uh-huh."

Susie uncrossed her legs and stood up. "Except you're not."

"Not what?"

"Coughing. Or sneezing."

"Well, it hit me differently, that's all."

"Have you been out of the country or something?"

"Not in weeks."

"I mean, there's all kinds of nasties floating around this old planet. Weren't you in Ghana or someplace like that a couple of months ago?"

"It was Kenya and it was last year, and honestly, I'm okay. You know what the flu can be like."

"Uh-huh." There was a long silence and then Susie cleared her throat. "My sister had the same symptoms last year. Nausea in the mornings, tossing her cookies every time somebody so much as mentioned food and generally looking just about as awful as you do.''

"Thanks a lot." Laurel speared her hands into her hair and shoved it off her forehead. Her skin felt clammy, and even though her stomach was completely empty, it still felt like a storm-tossed ship at sea. "Listen, Susie—"

"So she went to the doctor."

"I'm not going to the doctor. All I need is to take it easy for a couple of days and—"

"Turns out she was pregnant," Susie said quietly, her eyes on Laurel's face.

"Pregnant!" Laurel laughed. "Don't be silly, I'm not..."

Oh God! The floor seemed to drop out from beneath her feet.

Pregnant? No. It wasn't possible. Or was it? When had she last had her period? She couldn't remember. Was it since she'd been with Damian?

No. No!

She sank down on the edge of the bed, feeling empty and boneless. Everything had happened so quickly that night. Had Damian used a condom? Not that she could remember. She certainly hadn't used anything. Why take the pill, when sex was hardly a major item in your life? She knew some women carried diaphragms in their handbags but she wasn't one of them. You needed a whole different mind set to do that. You had to be the sort of woman who might find herself tumbling into a man's bed at the drop of a hat and she had never—she had certainly never...

A little sound tore from her throat. She looked at Susie's questioning face and did what she could to turn the sound into a choked laugh.

"I can't be," she said. "How could I possibly have gotten pregnant?"

"The method hasn't changed much through the centuries."

"Yes, but just one night..."

One night. One endless night.

"You need to make an appointment with your doctor," Susie said gently.

"No," Laurel whispered. She lifted her head and stared at Susie. "No," she said, more strongly. "It's ridiculous. I am not pregnant. I have the flu, that's all."

"I'm sure you're right," Susie said with a false smile. "But, what the heck, you want to make certain."

Laurel rose from the bed. "Look, how's this sound? I'll spend all day tomorrow in bed. I'll down aspirin and lots of liquids and if I'm not feeling better by Monday or Tuesday, I'll call my doctor."

"Your gynecologist."

"Really, Susie." Laurel looped her arm around the other woman's shoulders. Together, they headed for the foyer. "Give that imagination of yours a rest and I'll do the same for my flu-racked bones. And be sure and tell George I'm taking a rain check on dinner."

"I'm getting the brush-off, huh?"

"Well," Laurel said with forced gaiety, "if you want to hang around and listen to me upchuck again, you're welcome."

"Listen, if you need anything… Aspirin, Pepto-Bismol…" Susie flashed a quick smile. "Just someone to talk to, I'm here."

"Thanks, but I'm fine. Truly. You'll see. These bugs are all the same. You feel like dying for twenty-four hours and then you're as good as new."

"Didn't you say you'd been feeling shaky all week?"

"Twenty-four hours, forty-eight, what's the difference?" Laurel swung the door open. "It's flu, that's all. I'm not pregnant. Trust me."

"Uh-huh," Susie said, without conviction.

"I'm not," Laurel said firmly.

She held a smile until the door shut and she was safely alone. Then the smile faded and she sank back against the wall, eyes tightly shut. "I'm not," she whispered.

* * *

But she was.

Four weeks gone, Dr. Glassman said, later that afternoon, as Laurel sat opposite her in the gynecologist's sunny, plant-filled Manhattan office.

"I'm glad we could fit you in at the last minute like this, Laurel." The doctor smiled. "And I'm glad I can make such a certain diagnosis. You are with child."

With child. Damian's child.

"Have you married, since I saw you last?" A smile lit Dr. Glassman's pleasant, sixtyish face again. "Or have you decided, as is becoming so common, to have a child and remain single?"

Laurel licked her lips. "I—I'm still single."

"Ah. Well, you'll forgive me if I put on my obstetrical hat for a while and urge that you include your baby's father in his—or her—life, to as great a degree as possible." The doctor chuckled softly. "I know there are those who would have me drawn and quartered for saying such a thing, but children need two parents, whenever it's possible. A mother and a father, both."

There was no arguing with that, Laurel thought, oh, there was no arguing with—

"Any questions?"

Laurel cleared her throat. "No. None that I can think of just now, anyway."

"Well, that's it for today, then." The doctor took a card from a holder on her desk, scribbled something on it and handed it to Laurel. "Phone me Tuesday and I'll give you your lab reports, but I'm sure nothing unforeseen will arise. You're in excellent health, my dear. I see no reason why your baby shouldn't be healthy and full-term."

Dr. Glassman rose from her chair. Laurel did, too, but when the doctor smiled at her, she couldn't quite manage a smile in return.

"Laurel?" The doctor settled back behind her desk and peered over the rims of her reading glasses. "Of course," she said gently, "if you wish to make other arrangements..."

"I'm four weeks pregnant, you say?"

"Just about."

"And—and everything seems fine?"

"Perfectly fine."

Laurel gazed down at her hands, which were linked carefully in her lap. "If I should decide... I mean, if I were to..."

The doctor's voice was even more gentle. "You've plenty of time to think things through, my dear."

Laurel nodded and rose to her feet. Suddenly she felt a thousand years old.

"Thank you, Doctor."

The gynecologist rose, too. She came around her desk and put her arm lightly around Laurel's shoulders.

"I know what an enormous decision this is," she said. "If you need someone to talk to, my service can always reach me."

A baby, Laurel thought as she rode down in the elevator to the building's lobby. A child of her flesh. Hers, and Damian's.

Babies were supposed to be conceived in love, not in the throes of a passion that made no sense, a passion so out of character that she'd tried to put it out of her mind all these weeks. Not that she'd managed. In the merciless glare of daylight, she'd suddenly think of what she'd done and hate herself for it.

But at night, with the moonlight softening the shadows, she dreamed about Damian and awakened in a tangle of sheets, with the memory of his kisses still hot on her lips.

Laurel gave herself a little shake. This wasn't the time for that kind of nonsense. There were decisions to be made, although the only practical one was self-evident. There was no room in her life for a baby. Her apartment wasn't big enough. Her life was too unsettled, what with her career winding down and an uncertain future ahead. And then there was the biggest consideration of all. Dr. Glassman was right; some people might think it old-fashioned but it was true. Children were entitled to at least begin life with two parents.

The elevator door slid open and she stepped out into the lobby. Her high heels clicked sharply against the marble floor as she made her way toward the exit.

A baby. A soft, sweet-smelling, innocent bundle of smiles and gurgles. A child, to lavish love upon. To warm her heart and give purpose to her existence. Her throat constricted. A part of Damian that would be hers forever.

She paused outside the building, while an unseasonable wind ruffled her hair. Gum wrappers and a torn page from the *New York Times* flapped at her feet in the throes of a mini-tornado.

What was the point in torturing herself? She wasn't about to have this baby. Hadn't she already decided that? Her reasoning was sound; it was logical. It was—

"Laurel?"

Her heart stumbled. She knew the voice instantly; she'd heard it in her dreams a thousand times during the past long, tortured weeks. Still, she tried to tell herself that it couldn't be Damian. He was the last person she ever wanted to set eyes on again, especially now.

"Laurel."

Oh God, she thought, and she turned toward the curb and saw him stepping out of the same black limousine that had a month ago transported her from sanity to delirium. All at once, the wind seemed to grow stronger. Her vision blurred and she began to sway unsteadily.

And then she was falling, falling, and only Damian's arms could bring her to safety.

CHAPTER SEVEN

WHAT KIND OF MAN wanted a woman who'd made it clear she didn't want him?

Only a man who was a damned fool, and Damian had never counted himself as such.

And yet, four weeks after Laurel Bennett had slept in his arms and then walked out of his life, he had not been able to forget her.

He dreamed of her—hot, erotic dreams of the sort he'd left behind in adolescence. He thought of her during the least expected moments during the day, and when he'd tried to purge his mind and his flesh by becoming involved with someone else, it hadn't worked. He had wined and dined half a dozen of New York's most beautiful women during the past month, and every one had ended her evening puzzled, disappointed and alone.

It was stupid, and it angered him. He was not a man to waste time mourning lost opportunities or dreams. It was the philosophy that had guided his life since childhood; why should it fail him now? Laurel was what his financial people would have termed a write-off. She was a gorgeous woman with a hot body and an icy heart. She'd used him the way he'd used women in the past.

So how come he couldn't get her out of his head?

It was a question without an answer, and it was gnawing at him as his car pulled to the curb before the skyscraper that housed his corporate headquarters...which was why, when he first saw her, he wondered if he'd gone completely over the edge. But this was no hallucination. Laurel was real, she was coming out of the adjacent building—and she was even more beautiful than he'd remembered.

He stepped onto the sidewalk and hesitated. What now? Should he wait for her to notice him? He had nothing to say to her, really; still, he wanted to talk to her. Hell, he wanted more than that. He wanted to go to her, take her in his arms, run his thumb along her bottom lip until her mouth opened to his…

Damian frowned. What was this? The feverish glow on her cheeks couldn't hide the fact that her face was pale. She seemed hesitant, just standing there while pedestrians flowed around her like a stream of water against an immutable rock.

Dammit, she was weeping!

He started toward her. "Laurel?"

She had to be ill. She'd never cry, otherwise; he knew it instinctively. His belly knotted.

"Laurel," he shouted, and she looked up and saw him.

For one wild, heart-stopping instant, he thought he saw her face light with joy but he knew it had only been his imagination because a second later her eyes widened, her pallor became waxy and she mouthed his name as if it were an obscenity.

His mouth thinned. To hell with her, then…

God, she was collapsing!

"Laurel," Damian roared, and he dove through the crowd and snatched her up in his arms just before she fell.

She made a little sound as he gathered her close to him.

"It's all right," he whispered, "I've got you, Laurel. It's okay."

Her lashes fluttered. She looked at him but he could tell she wasn't really focusing. His arms tightened around her and he pressed his lips to her hair while his heart thundered in his chest. What if he hadn't been here, to catch her? What if she'd fallen?

What if he'd never held her in his arms again?

"Damian?" she whispered.

There was a breathy little catch in her voice, and it tore at his heart. She sounded as fragile as Venetian glass. She felt that way, too. She was tall for a woman and he would never have thought of her as delicate yet now, in his arms, that was how she seemed.

"Damian? What happened?"

"How in hell should I know!" The words sounded uncaring. He hadn't meant them to be, it was just that a dozen emotions were warring inside him and he didn't understand a one of them. "I was just getting out of my car... You fainted."

"Fainted? Me?" He watched the tip of her tongue slick across her lips. "Don't be silly. I've never passed out in my..." Color flooded her face as she remembered. The doctor. The diagnosis. "Oh God," she whispered, and squeezed her eyes shut.

Damian frowned. "What is it? Are you going to pass out again?"

She took a deep breath and forced herself to open her eyes. Damian looked angry. Well, why not? He'd never expected to see her again and now here he was, standing on a crowded street with her in his arms, playing an unwilling Sir Galahad to her damsel in distress and, dammit, *he* was the reason for that distress. If she'd never laid eyes on him, never gone to dinner with him, never let herself be seduced by him...

It wasn't true. He hadn't seduced her. She'd gone to bed with him willingly. Eagerly. Even now, knowing that her world would never be the same again no matter what she decided, even now, lying in his arms, she felt—she felt—

She stiffened, and put her palms flat against his chest.

"I'm not going to pass out again, no. I'm fine, as a matter of fact. Please put me down."

"I don't think so."

"Don't be ridiculous!" People hurrying past were looking at them with open curiosity. Even in New York, a man standing in the middle of a crowded sidewalk with a woman in his arms was bound to attract attention. "Damian, I said—"

"I heard what you said." The crowd gave way, not much and not very gracefully, but Damian gave it no choice. "Coming through," he barked, and Laurel caught her breath as she realized he was carrying her back into the building she'd just left.

"What are you doing?"

"There must be a dozen doctors' offices in this building. We'll pick the first one and—"

"No!" Panic surged through her with the speed of adrenaline. "I don't need a doctor!"

"Of course you do. People don't pass out cold for no reason."

"But there was a reason. I—I've been dieting." It was the same lie she'd tried on Susie hours ago, but this time, she knew it would work. "Nothing but tomato juice and black coffee for breakfast, lunch and dinner," she said, rattling off the latest lose-weight-quick scheme that was floating through the fashion world. "You can drop five pounds in two days."

Five pounds? Damian couldn't imagine why she'd want to lose an ounce. She felt perfect to him, warm and lushly curved, just as she'd been in his dreams each night.

"You don't need to lose five pounds."

"The camera doesn't agree."

His smile was quick and dangerously sexy. "Maybe the camera hasn't had as intimate a view of you as I have."

Laurel stiffened in his arms. "How nice to know you're still the perfect gentleman. For the last time, Damian. Put me down!"

His eyes narrowed at the coldness of her voice. "My pleasure." He put her on her feet but he kept a hand clamped around her elbow. "Let's go."

"Go? Go where? Dammit, Damian…"

She sputtered with indignation as he hustled her through the door, across the sidewalk and toward the limousine. Stevens was already out of the front seat, standing beside the rear door and holding it open, his face a polite mask as if he were accustomed to seeing his employer snatch women off the street.

Laurel dug in her heels but it was useless. Damian was strong, and determined, and even when she called him a word that made his eyebrows lift, he didn't loosen his hold.

"Thank you, Stevens," he said smoothly. "Get into the car please, Laurel."

Get into the car, *please?* He made it sound like a polite request, but a request was something you could turn down. This was a command. Despite her struggles, her protests, her locked knees and gritted teeth, Damian was herding her onto the leather seat.

She swung toward him, eyes blazing, as he settled himself alongside her.

"How *dare* you? How dare you treat me this way? I am not some—some package to be dumped in a truck and—and shipped off."

"No," he said coldly, "you are not. You're a pigheaded female, apparently bent on seeing which you can manage first, starving yourself to death or giving yourself a concussion." The car nosed into the stream of traffic moving sluggishly up the avenue. "Well, I'm going to take you home. Then, for all I give a damn, you can gorge on tomato soup and black coffee while you practice swan dives on the living-room floor."

"It's tomato juice," Laurel said furiously, "not soup. And I was not doing swan dives." She glared at Damian. Her skirt was rucked up, her hair was hanging in her eyes, a button had popped off her knit dress and there he sat, as cool as ice, with a look on his face that said he was far superior to other human beings. How she hated this man!

"A perfect three-pointer," he said, "aimed right at the pavement."

"Will you stop that? I just—I felt a little light-headed, that's all."

"At the sight of me," he said, fixing her with a stony look.

Laurel flushed. "Don't flatter yourself."

"Tomato juice and black coffee," he growled. "It's a toss-up which you are, light-brained or light-headed."

Laurel glared at him. She blew a strand of hair off her forehead, folded her arms in unwitting parody of him and they rode through the streets in silence. When they reached her apartment house, she sprang for the door before Damian could move or Stevens could get out of the car.

"Thank you so much for the lift," she said, her words dripping with venom. "I wish I could say it's been a pleasure seeing you, but what's the sense in lying?"

"Such sweet words, Laurel. I'm touched." Damian looked up at her and a half smile curled over his mouth. "Remember what I said. You don't need to lose any weight."

"Advice from an expert," she said, with a poisonous smile.

"Try some real food for a change."

"What are you, a nutritionist?"

"Of course, you could always get back into the car."

"In your dreams," she said, swinging away from him.

"We could go back to the *Penthouse*. Maybe you'd like to see what you missed last time. The caviar, the duck, the soufflé…"

Caviar, oily and salty. Duck, with the fat melting under the skin. Chocolate soufflé, under a mantle of whipped cream…

Laurel's stomach lifted. No, she thought, oh please, no…

The little she had eaten since the morning bolted up her throat.

Dimly, over the sound of her retching, she heard Damian's soft curse. Then his hands were clasping her shoulders, supporting her as her belly sought to do the impossible and turn itself inside-out. When the spasms passed, he pulled her back against him. She went willingly, mortified by shame but weak in body and in spirit, desperately needing the comfort he offered.

"I'm so sorry," she whispered.

Damian turned her toward him. He took out his handkerchief and gently wiped her clammy forehead and her mouth. Then he swung her into his arms and carried her inside the house.

She was beyond protest. When he asked for her keys, she handed him her pocketbook. When he settled her on the living-room couch, she fell back against the cushions. He took off her shoes, undid the top buttons on her dress, tucked a pillow under her head and an afghan over her legs and warned her not to move.

Move? She'd have laughed, if she'd had the strength. As it was, she could barely nod her head.

Damian took off his jacket, tossed it over a chair and headed for the kitchen. She heard the fridge opening and she wondered what he'd think when he saw the contents. Her seesawing stomach had kept her from doing much shopping or cooking lately.

Laurel swallowed. Better not to think about food. With luck, there just might be some ginger ale on the shelf, or some Diet Coke.

"Ginger ale," Damian said. He squatted down beside her, put his arm around her shoulders and eased her head up. "It's flat, but that's just as well. Slowly, now. One sip at a time."

Another command, but she still didn't have the energy to argue. Anyway, it was good advice. She didn't want to be sick again, not with Damian here.

"There's a chemistry experiment in your kitchen," he said.

"A chem...?"

"Either that, or an alien presence has landed on the counter near the sink."

Laurel laughed weakly and lay back against the pillow. "It's sourdough."

"Ah. Well, I hope you don't mind, but I've disposed of

it. I had the uncomfortable feeling it was planning on taking over the apartment.''

"Thanks."

"How do you feel now?"

"Better." She sighed deeply, yawned and found herself fighting to keep her eyes open. "I must have eaten something that disagreed with me."

"Close your eyes," he said. "Rest for a while."

"I'm not tired."

"Yes, you are."

"For heaven's sake, Damian, must you pretend you know every…"

Her eyes closed. She was asleep.

Damian rose to his feet. No, he thought grimly, he didn't know everything, but he knew enough to figure that a woman who claimed she'd been on a diet of tomato juice and black coffee wasn't very likely to have eaten something that made her sick…especially not when she was carrying around a little white card like the one that had fallen from her pocket when he'd put her on the couch.

He walked into the kitchen and took the card from the table, where he'd left it: Vivian Glassman, M.D., Gynecology and Obstetrics.

It probably didn't mean a thing. People tucked away cards and forgot about them, and even if that was where Laurel had been today, what did it prove? Women went for gynecological checkups regularly.

His fist clenched around the card. He thought of Laurel's face, when she'd seen him coming toward her a little while ago—and he thought of something else.

All these weeks that he'd dreamed of her, relived the night they'd spent in each other's arms. The heat, the sweetness—all of it had seemed permanently etched into his brain. Now, another memory vied for his attention, one that made his belly cramp.

In all that long, wild night, he'd never thought to use a condom.

It was so crazy, so irresponsible, so completely unlike him. It was as if he'd been intoxicated that night, drunk on the smell of Laurel's skin and the taste of her mouth.

He hadn't used a condom. She hadn't used a diaphragm. Now she was nauseous, and faint, and she was seeing a doctor whose specialty was obstetrics.

Maybe she was on the pill. Maybe his imagination was in overdrive.

Maybe it was time to get some answers.

He took a long, harsh breath. Then he reached for the phone.

Laurel awoke slowly.

She was lying on the living-room couch. Darkness had gathered outside the windows but someone had turned on the table lamp.

Someone?

Damian.

He was sitting in a chair a few feet away. There was a granitelike set to his jaw; above it, his mouth was set in a harsh line.

"How do you feel?"

She swallowed experimentally. Her stomach growled, but it stayed put.

"Much better." She sat up, pushed the afghan aside and swung her legs to the floor. "Thank you for everything, Damian, but there really wasn't any need for you to sit here while I slept." He said nothing, and the silence beat in her ears. Something was wrong, she could feel it. "What time is it, anyway?" she asked, trying for a light tone. "I must have slept for—"

"When did you plan on telling me?"

Her heart thumped, then lodged like a stone behind her breastbone.

"Plan on telling you what?" She rose to her feet and he did, too, and came toward her. Damn, where were her shoes? He was so tall. It put her at a disadvantage, to let him loom over her like this.

"Perhaps you didn't intend to tell me." His voice hummed with challenge; his accent thickened. "Was that your plan?"

"I don't know what you're talking about," she said, starting past him, "and I'm really not in the mood for games."

"And I," he said, clamping his hand down on her shoulder, "am not in the mood for lies."

Her eyes flashed fire as she swung toward him. "I think you'd better leave."

"You're pregnant," he said flatly.

Pregnant. Pregnant. The word seemed to echo through the room.

"I don't know what you're talking about."

"It will be easier if you tell me the truth."

She twisted free of his grasp and pointed at the door. "It will be easier if you get out of here."

"Is the child mine?"

"Is...?" Laurel stuffed her hands into her pockets. "There is no child. I don't know where you got this idea, but—"

"How many men were you with that week, aside from me?"

"Get out, damn you!"

"I ask you again, is the child mine?"

She stared at him, her lips trembling. No, she wanted to say, it is not. I was with a dozen men that week. A hundred. A thousand.

"Answer me!" His hands clamped around her shoulders and he shook her roughly. "Is it mine?"

In the end, it was too barbarous a lie to tell.

"Yes," she whispered, "it's yours."

He said nothing for a long moment. Then he jerked his head towards the sofa.

"Sit down, Laurel."

She looked up and their eyes met. A shudder raced through her. She stepped back, until she felt the edge of the sofa behind her, and then she collapsed onto the cushions like a rag doll.

"How—how did you find out?"

His mouth curled. He reached into his pocket, took out a small white card and tossed it into her lap. Laurel stared down at it. It was the card Dr. Glassman had given her.

She looked up at him. "She told you? Dr. Glassman *told* you? She had no right! She—"

"She told me nothing." His mouth twisted again. "And everything."

"I don't understand."

"The card fell from your pocket. I telephoned Glassman's office. The receptionist put me through when I said I was a 'friend' of yours and concerned about your health."

The twist he put on the word brought a rush of color to Laurel's face. Damian saw it and flashed a thin smile.

"Apparently your physician made the same interpretation. But she was very discreet. She acknowledged only that she knew you. She said I would have to discuss your medical condition with you, and she hung up."

Laurel's face whitened. "Then—then you didn't really know! You lied to me. You fooled me into—into—"

"I put two and two together, that's all, and then I asked a question, which you answered."

"It wasn't a question!" Laurel drew a shuddering breath. "You said you knew that I was—that I was—"

"I asked if it was my child." He moved suddenly, bending down and spearing his arms on either side of her, trapping her, pinning her with a look that threatened to turn her to ice. "My child, damn you! What were you planning, Laurel? To give it up for adoption? To have it aborted?"

"No!" The cry burst from her throat and, as it did, she knew that it was the truth. She would not give up the life within her. She wanted her baby, with all her heart and soul, had wanted it from the moment the doctor had confirmed that she was pregnant. "No," she whispered, her gaze steady on his. "I'm not going to do that. I'm going to have my baby, and keep it."

"Keep it?" Damian's mouth twisted. "This is not a puppy we speak of. How will you keep it? How will you raise a child alone?"

"You'd be amazed at how much progress women have made," Laurel said defiantly. "We're capable of rearing children as well as giving birth to them."

"A child will interfere with the self-indulgent life you lead."

"You don't know the first thing about my life!"

"I know that a woman who sleeps with strangers cannot possibly pretend to be a fit mother for my child."

Laurel slammed her fist into his shoulder. "What a hypocritical son of a bitch you are! Who are you to judge me? It took two of us to create this baby, Damian, two strangers in one bed that night!"

A thin smile touched his lips. "It is not the same."

"It is not the same," she said, cruelly mimicking his tone and his accent. She rose and shoved past him. "Do us both a favor, will you? Get out of here. Get out of my life. I don't ever want to see your face again!"

"I would do so, and gladly, but you forget that this life you carry belongs to me."

"It's a baby, Damian. You don't own a baby. I suppose that's hard for someone like you to comprehend, but a child's not a—a commodity. You can't own it, even if your name is Damian Skouras."

They glared at each other, and then he muttered something in Greek and stalked away from her.

Dammit, she was right! He was behaving like an ass. That self-righteous crap a minute ago, about a woman who slept with strangers not being a fit mother, was ridiculous. He was as responsible for what had happened as she was.

And now she was carrying a child. His child. A deep

warmth suffused his blood. He had always thought raising Nick would be the closest he'd come to fatherhood. Now, Fate and a woman who'd haunted his dreams had joined forces to show him another way.

Slowly, he turned and looked at Laurel.

"I want my child," he said softly.

Laurel went cold. "What do you mean, you want your child?"

"I mean exactly what I said. This child is mine, and I will not forfeit my claim to it."

His claim? She felt her legs turn to jelly. This kind of thing cropped up in the papers and on TV news shows, reports of fathers who demanded, and won, custody. Not many, it was true, but this was Damian Skouras, who had all the power and wealth in the world. He could take her baby from her with a snap of his fingers.

Be calm, she told herself, be calm, and don't let him see how frightened you are.

"Do you understand, Laurel?"

"Yes. I understand." She made her way toward him, her gaze locked on his face, assessing what to offer and what to hold back, wondering how you played poker with a man who owned all the chips. "Look, Damian, let's not discuss this now, when we're both upset."

"There is nothing to discuss. I'm telling you how it will be. I will be a father to my child."

"Well, I'm not—I'm not opposed to you having a role in this. In fact, Dr. Glassman and I talked a little bit about— about the value of a father, in a child's life. I'm sure we can work out some sort of agreement."

"Visiting rights?"

"Yes."

His smile was even more frightening the second time. "How generous of you, Laurel."

"I'm sure we can work out an arrangement that will suit us both."

"Did I ever tell you that my father played no part in my life?"

"Look, I don't know what the situation was between your parents, but—"

"I might as well have been a bastard."

"Damian—"

"I have no great confidence in marriage, I assure you, but when children are involved, I have even less in divorce."

"Well, this wouldn't be the same situation at all," she said, trying not to sound as desperate as she felt. "I mean, since we wouldn't be married, there'd be no divorce to worry ab—"

"My child deserves better. He—or she—is entitled to two parents, and to stability."

"I think so, too," she said quickly. "That's why I'd be willing to—to permit you a role."

"To permit me?" he said, so softly that she knew her choice of words had been an error.

"I didn't mean that the way it sounded. I won't keep you from my—from our—child. I swear it."

"You swear," he said, his tone mocking hers. "How touching. Am I to take comfort in the word of a woman who didn't even intend to tell me she was pregnant?"

"Dammit, what do you want? Just tell me!"

"I *am* telling you. I will not abandon my child, nor be a father in name only, and I have no intention of putting my faith in agreements reached by greedy lawyers."

"That's fine." She gave him a dazzling smile. "No lawyers, then. No judges. We'll sit down, like two civilized people, and work out an arrangement that will suit us both." She cried out sharply as his hands bit into her flesh. "Damian, you're hurting me!"

"Do you take me for a fool?" He leaned toward her, so that his face was only inches from hers. "I can imagine the sort of arrangement you would wish."

"You're wrong. I just agreed, didn't I, that a father has a place in a child's life?"

"Ten minutes ago, you were telling me you never wanted to see my face again."

"Yes, but that was before I understood how deeply you feel about this."

"You mean, it was before you were trapped into telling me you were pregnant." He laughed. "You're a bad liar, Laurel."

"Damn you, Damian! What do you want from me?"

There was a long, heavy silence. Then his arms wound around her and his hands slipped into her hair.

"Don't," she said, but already his mouth was dropping to hers, taking it in a kiss that threatened to steal her sanity. When, finally, he drew back, Laurel was trembling. With hatred, with rage—and with the shattering knowledge that, even now, his kiss could still make her want him.

"I have always believed," he said softly, "that a man should have children only within the sanctity of marriage. But that is a paradox, because I believe that marriage is a farce. Nonetheless, I see no choice here." His hand lifted, as if to touch her hair, then fell to his side. "We will marry within the week."

"We will...?" She felt the blood drain from her face. "Marry? Did you say, *marry*?"

"We will marry, and we will have our child, and we will raise him—or her—together."

"You're crazy! Me, marry you? Never! Do you hear me? Not in a million years would—"

"You've accused me of being arrogant, and egocentric. Well, I assure you, I can be those things, and more." A muscle beside his mouth tightened, and his eyes bored into hers. "I am Damian Skouras. I command resources you'll never dream of. Oppose me, and all you'll gain is ugly notoriety for yourself, your family and our child."

Laurel began to tremble. She stared back at him and then

she wrenched free. Angry tears blurred her eyes and she wiped them away with a slash of her hand.

"I hate you, Damian! I'll always hate you!"

He laughed softly, reached for his jacket and slung it over one shoulder.

"That's quite all right, dearest Laurel. From what I know of matrimony, that's the natural state of things."

Damian opened the door and walked out.

CHAPTER EIGHT

FIVE DAYS LATER, they stood as far apart as they could manage in the anteroom to a judge's chambers in a town just north of the city.

Judge Weiss was a friend of a friend, Damian had said. He'd begun to explain the connection, but Laurel had stopped him halfway through.

"It doesn't matter," she'd said stiffly.

And it didn't. For all she gave a damn, the man who was about to marry them could be an insurance salesman who was a justice of the peace in his spare time.

The only thing she wanted now was to get the thing over with.

She hadn't asked anyone to attend the ceremony. She hadn't told Susie or George or even Annie that she was getting married. Her sister had seemed preoccupied lately and anyway, what was there to tell? Surely not the truth, that she'd made the oldest, saddest female blunder in the world and that now she was paying the classic price for it by marrying a man she didn't love.

She'd decided it would be better to break the news when this was all over. She'd make it sound as if she and Damian had followed through on a romantic, spur-of-the-moment impulse. Susie might see through it but Annie, good-hearted soul that she was, would probably be thrilled.

She glanced over at Damian. He was standing with his back to her, staring out the window. He'd been doing that for the past ten minutes, as if the traffic passing by on the road outside was so fascinating that he couldn't tear his gaze from it.

She understood it, because she had been staring at a bad

111

oil painting of a man in judicial robes with mutton-chop whiskers for the same reason. It was a way of focusing on something other than the reality of what was about to happen.

Laurel took a deep breath. There was still time. Maybe she could convince him that his plan was crazy, that it was no good for him or her or even for their baby.

"Mr. Skouras? Miss Bennett?"

Laurel and Damian both looked around. The door to the judge's office had opened. A small, gray-haired woman smiled pleasantly at them.

"Judge Weiss is ready for you now," she said.

Laurel's hands tightened on her purse. It was like being told the dentist was ready for you. Your heart rate speeded up, your skin got clammy, you had to tell yourself to smile back and act as if that was exactly the wonderful news you'd been waiting for.

Except this wasn't the dentist's office, and she wasn't going to have a tooth drilled. She was going to hand her life over to Damian Skouras.

"Laurel."

She looked up. Damian was coming toward her, his expression grim.

"The judge is ready."

"I heard." She swallowed hard against a sudden rise of nausea, not from the pregnancy—that had ended, strangely enough, the day Damian had learned of her condition. This churning in her gut had to do with the step she was about to take.

I can't. God, I can't.

"Damian." She took a deep breath. "Damian, listen. I think we ought to talk."

His hand closed around hers, tightening in warning, and he smiled pleasantly at the clerk.

"Thank you. Please tell the judge we'll be along in a minute."

As soon as the door swung shut, Damian turned back to Laurel, his eyes cold.

"We have discussed this. There is nothing more to be said."

"We've discussed nothing! You've issued edicts and I've bowed my head in obedience. Well, now I'm telling you that it isn't going to work. I don't think—"

"I haven't asked you to think."

Color flew into her cheeks. "If *you'd* been thinking, we wouldn't be in this mess!"

It was an unfair attack, and she knew it. She was as responsible for what had happened as Damian, but why should she play fair when he didn't? Still, he didn't deny the accusation.

"Yes." A muscle tightened in his jaw. "You are correct. We are in, as you say, a mess, and since it is one of my own making, the solution is mine, as well. There is no other course to take."

"No other course that meets with your approval, you mean." She tried to shake off his hand, but he wouldn't let her. "If you'd be reasonable—"

"Meaning that I should permit you to do as you see fit?"

"Yes. No. Will you stop twisting everything I say? If you'd just think for a minute... We have nothing in common. We hardly know each other. We don't even like each other, and yet—and yet, you expect me to—to marry you, to become your wife."

"I expect exactly that."

Laurel yanked her hand from his. "Damn you," she whispered. She was trembling with rage, at Damian, at herself, at a situation that had gotten out of control and had brought this nightmare down on her head. "Damn you, Damian! You have an answer for everything and it's the same each time. You know best, you know what's right, you know how things have to be—"

Behind them, the door swung open.

"Mr. Skouras? The judge has a busy schedule this morning. If you and Miss Bennett wouldn't mind...?"

Miss Bennett minds, very much, Laurel thought...but Damian's hand had already closed around hers.

"Of course," he said, with a soft-as-butter smile that had nothing to do with the steely pressure of his fingers. "Darling? Are you ready?"

His smile was soft, too, but the warning in his eyes left no room for doubt. Make no mistake, he was telling her; do as I say or suffer the consequences.

Laurel gathered what remained of her self-composure, lifted her chin and nodded.

"As ready as I can be," she said coolly, and let him lead her into the judge's office.

It was a large, masculine room, furnished in heavy mahogany. The walls were paneled with some equally dark wood and hung with framed clippings and photos of politicos ranging from John F. Kennedy to Bill Clinton. Someone, perhaps the clerk, had tucked a bouquet of flowers into a coffee mug and placed it on the mantel above the fireplace, but the flowers weren't fresh and their drooping heads and faded colors only added a mournful touch to the room. An ancient air conditioner wheezed in the bottom half of a smeared window as it tried to breathe freshness into air redolent with the smell of old cigars.

"Mr. Skouras," the judge said, rising from behind his desk and smiling, "and Miss Bennett. What a fine day for a wedding."

It was, Laurel supposed. Outside, the sun was shining brightly; puffy white clouds sailed across a pale blue sky.

But weddings weren't supposed to be held in stuffy rooms like this one. A woman dreamed of being married in a place filled with light; she dreamed of flowers and friends around her, and of coming to her groom with a heart filled with joy and love.

If only this were real. If only Damian truly wanted her, and loved her...

A sound of distress burst from Laurel's throat. She took a quick step back. Instantly Damian's arm slid around her waist.

"Laurel?" he said softly.

She looked up at him, her eyes dark and glistening with unshed tears, and he felt as if a fist had clamped around his heart.

She didn't want this. He knew that, but it didn't matter. He'd told himself that a dozen times over. The child. That was the only thing that mattered. They had to marry, for the sake of the child. It was the right thing to do.

Now, looking down into the eyes of his bride, seeing the sorrow shimmering in their depths, Damian felt a twinge of uncertainty.

Was Laurel right? Was this a mistake?

She had offered to share the raising of their child with him, and he had scoffed. And with good cause. It didn't take a genius to see that what she really wanted was to get him out of her life forever. Still, a clever attorney could have made that an impossibility and he had a team of the best. A child should be raised by two parents; his belief in that would never change. But what good could come of being raised by a mother and father who lived in a state of armed truce?

Why, then, was he forcing this marriage?

Why was he taking as his wife a woman who hated him so much that she was on the verge of weeping? Damian's throat tightened. This wasn't the way it should be. A man wanted his bride to look up at him and smile; he wanted to see joy shining in her eyes as they were joined together.

If only, just for a little while, Laurel could look as if she wanted him. As if she remembered how it had been, that night...

"...always beautiful but you, my dear Miss Bennett, are a treat for an old man's eyes. And Mr. Skouras." The judge, a big man with a belly and a voice to match, clasped Damian's hand and shook it heartily. "I know you by rep-

utation, of course. It is a pleasure to meet you, and to of-
ficiate at your wedding.''

Damian cleared his throat. ''Thank you for fitting us into
your schedule, Your Honor. I know how difficult it must
have been, but everything was so last minute...''

Judge Weiss laughed. ''Elopements generally are, my
boy.'' He smiled, rubbed his hands together and reached
for a small, battered black book. ''Well, shall we begin?''

''No!'' Laurel's cry was as sharp as broken glass. The
judge's smile faded as he looked at her.

''I beg your pardon? Is there a problem, Miss Bennett?''

''There is no problem,'' Damian said smoothly. ''We
made our decision so quickly...my fiancée is simply having
a last-minute attack of nerves, Your Honor.'' Damian slid
his arm around Laurel's waist. She looked up at him and
he smiled. It was an affectionate smile, just as the way he
was holding her seemed affectionate, but she knew better.
''I suppose,'' he said, flashing the judge a just-between-us-
boys grin that made the older man chuckle, ''I suppose that
no bride is calm on her wedding day.''

''Damian,'' Laurel said, ''it isn't too late—''

''Hush,'' he whispered, and before she could stop him,
he tilted her chin up and kissed her.

It was a quick, gentle kiss, nothing more than the lightest
brush of his mouth against hers, and she wondered, later,
if that had been her undoing. Perhaps if he'd kissed her
harder, if he'd tried, with silken tongue and teasing teeth,
to remind her of the passion that had once consumed them,
everything would have ended in that instant.

But he didn't. He kissed her the way a man kisses a
woman he truly loves, with a sweet tenderness that numbed
her senses.

''Everything will be fine, *kalí mou*,'' he murmured. He
lifted her hand to his lips, pressed a kiss to the palm and
sealed her fingers over it. ''Trust me.''

The judge cleared his throat. ''Well,'' he said briskly,
''are we ready now?''

"Ready," Damian said, and so it began.

The words were not as flowery, but neither were they very different from the ones that had been spoken in the little Connecticut church, barely more than four weeks before. The sentiments were surely the same; the judge had told Damian, over the phone, that he prided himself on offering a little ceremony of his own creation to each couple he wed.

He spoke of friendship, and of love. Of the importance of not taking vows lightly. Of commitment, and respect.

And, at last, he intoned the words Laurel had been dreading.

"Do you, Laurel Bennett, take Damian Skouras to be your lawfully wedded husband?"

A lump seemed to have lodged in her throat. She tried to swallow past it. The judge, and Damian, were looking at her.

"I'm sorry," she said, stalling for time, "I didn't—I didn't hear…"

The judge smiled. "I asked if you were prepared to take Damian Skouras as your lawfully wedded husband."

"Miss Bennett?"

Laurel shut her eyes. She thought of her baby, and of the power Damian held…and then, though it was stupid and pointless, because she didn't love him, didn't even like him, she thought of the way he'd kissed her only moments ago…

She took a shaky breath, opened her eyes and said, "Yes."

The car was waiting outside.

"Congratulations, sir," Stevens said, as he opened the door. He looked at Laurel and smiled. "And my best wishes to you, too, madam."

Best wishes? On an occasion such as this? Laurel felt like laughing. Or weeping. Or maybe both but then, the chauffeur was as much in the dark about this marriage as everybody else.

It wasn't easy, but she managed to summon up a smile. "Thank you, Stevens."

Damian seemed to find that amusing.

"Nicely done," he said, as the car swung out into traffic. "I'd half expected you to assure Stevens that you were being carried off against your will."

Laurel folded her hands in her lap and stared straight ahead.

"Stevens was just being polite, and I responded in kind. I can hardly hold him responsible for the dilemma I'm in."

"The dilemma you're in?"

There was a soft note of warning in his voice, but Laurel chose to ignore it.

"We're alone now, Damian. The judge isn't here to watch our performance. If you expect me to pretend, you're in for an unpleasant surprise."

"I refer to your attitude toward my child. I will not have it thought of as a dilemma."

"You're twisting my words again. This travesty of a marriage is what I meant. I want this baby, and you damn well know it. Otherwise I wouldn't be sitting here, pretending that—that all that mumbo jumbo we just went through is real."

"Pretending?" His lips compressed into a tight smile. "There's no pretense in this. I have a document in my pocket that attests to the legitimacy of our union. You are my wife, Laurel, and I am your husband."

"Never!" The words she'd kept bottled inside tumbled from her lips. "Do you hear me, Damian? In my heart, where it matters, you'll never be my husband!"

"Such a sharp tongue, sweetheart." He shifted in his seat so that he was leaning toward her, his face only inches away. "And such empty threats."

"It isn't a threat." She could feel her pulse beating like a fist in her throat. "It's a statement of fact. You may have been able to force me into this marriage but you can't change what I feel."

He touched the back of his hand to her cheek, then drew his fingers slowly into her hair. The pins that held it up worked loose and it started to come undone, but when she lifted her hand to fix it, he stopped her.

"Leave it," he said softly.

"It's—it's messy."

He smiled. "It's beautiful, and it's how I prefer it."

It was difficult to breathe, with him so close. She thought of putting her hands against his chest and pushing him away, but then she thought of that night, that fateful night, and how they'd ridden in this car and how she'd wound her arms tightly around his neck and kissed him...

...how she longed to kiss him, even now.

God. Oh God, what was happening to her?

"Really," she said, with a forced little laugh, "how I wear my hair is none of your business."

"You are my wife." He ran his hand the length of her throat. Her pulse fluttered under his fingers like a trapped bird, confirming what he already suspected, that though his bride seemed to have recovered her composure, she was not quite as calm as she wanted him to believe. "Is the thought so difficult to bear?"

"I learned something, when I was first starting in modeling. I never asked a question unless I was sure I wanted to hear the answer."

He stroked his thumb across the fullness of her bottom lip. A tremor went through her, and her eyes darkened.

"Don't," she whispered—but her lips parted and her breathing quickened.

His body quickened, too. She wanted him, despite everything she'd said. He could read it in the blurring of her eyes, in the softening of her mouth.

Now, he thought. He could have her now, in his arms, returning his kisses, sighing her acquiescence against his skin as he undressed her.

He bent his head, pressed his mouth to the slender column of her throat. She smelled of sunshine and flowers, summer and rain. He shut his eyes, nuzzled her collar aside and kissed her skin. It was softer than any silk, and as warm as fresh honey.

"Laurel," he whispered, and he drew back and looked into her face. Her eyes were wide with confusion and dark with desire, and a fierce sense of joy swept through him.

He ran his thumb over her mouth again. Again, her lips parted and this time, he dipped into the heat that awaited him. A soft moan broke from her throat and he felt the quick flutter of her tongue against his finger. Her hands lifted, pressed against his shoulders, then rose to encircle his neck. Damian groaned and pressed her back into the seat.

God, how he wanted her! And he could take her. She was his wife, and she wanted him. She was a sensual, sexual woman and now there would be no other men for her.

What choice did she have, but to want him?

He pulled away from her so quickly that she fell back against the leather seat.

"You see?" he said, and smiled coldly. "It will not be so bad, to be my wife."

Her face reddened. "I hope you go to hell," she said, in a voice that trembled, and as he turned his face and stared out the window at the landscape rushing by, he wondered what she would say if he told her that he was starting to think he was already there.

He had to give her credit.

He had told her they'd be leaving the country but she didn't ask any questions, not where they were going, or why, and she didn't blink an eye when they boarded a sleek private jet with Skouras International discreetly stenciled on the fuselage.

She settled into a seat, buckled her seat belt, plucked a magazine from the table beside her and buried her nose in it, never looking up or speaking except to decline, politely, when the steward asked if she'd like lunch.

But not even an actress as good as Laurel could keep up the deception forever. Four hours into the flight, she finally put the magazine down and stirred.

"Is it a matter of control?" she said. "Or did you just want to see how long it would take me to ask?"

He looked up from his laptop computer and the file he'd been pretending to read and smiled politely.

"Pardon?"

"Stop playing games, Damian. Where are we going?"

He took his time replying, signing off the file, shutting down the computer, stuffing it back into its leather case and laying it aside before he looked at her.

"Out of the country. I told you that yesterday."

"You told me you had business to attend to and to bring along my passport. But we've been flying for hours and—" *and I'm frightened* "—and now, I'm asking you where you're taking me."

"Greece," he said, almost lazily.

His answer shocked her. She'd been to Greece once; she remembered its stark beauty as well as the feeling that had come over her, as if she'd stumbled into another time when the old rules that governed behavior between the sexes were very different than they were now.

"Greece?" she said, trying not to let her growing apprehension show. "But why?"

"Why not?"

"I'm not in the mood for games, Damian. I asked a question, and I'd like an answer. Why are we going to Greece?"

There were half a dozen answers to give her, all of them reasonable and all of them true.

Because I own an island there, he could have said, and there was a storm last month and now I want to check on my property. Because I have business interests on Crete, and those, too, need checking. Because I like the hot sun and the sapphire water...

"Because it is where I was born," he said simply, and waited.

Her reaction was swift and not anything he'd expected.

"I do not want my child born in Greece," she said hotly. "He—or she—is going to be an American citizen."

Damian laughed softly. "As am I, dearest wife, I assure you."

"Then why...?"

"I thought it would be a place where we could be free of distraction while we get to know each other."

Catlike, he stretched. He'd taken off his jacket and tie, undone the top two buttons of his shirt and folded back the sleeves. His skin gleamed golden in the muted cabin light, his muscles flexed. Laurel felt a fine tremor dance down her spine. Whatever else she thought of him, there was no denying that he was a beautiful sight to behold.

And now, he was hers. He was her husband. The night she'd spent in his arms could be a night lived over again, on the sands beside a midnight sea or on a wild hilltop with the sun beating down on the both of them. She could kiss Damian's mouth and run her hands over his skin, whisper his name as he pleasured her...

Panic roughened her voice.

"I don't want to go to Greece, dammit! Didn't it ever occur to you to consult me before you made these plans?"

Damian looked at his wife's face. Her eyes glittered, with an emotion he could not define.

Fear. She was terrified, and of him.

God, why was he being such a mean son of a bitch? He had forced her into this marriage for the best of reasons but that didn't mean he had to treat her so badly. She was right, he should have consulted her. He should have told her, anyway, that he was taking her to Greece, to his island, Actos. He should have told her that for some reason he couldn't fathom, he wanted her to see where he had lost the boy he'd been and found the man he'd become.

He felt a tightening inside him, not just in his belly but in his heart.

"Laurel," he said, and touched her shoulder.

She flinched as if she'd been scalded.

"Don't touch me," she snarled, and he pulled back his hand, his face hardening, and thought that the place he was taking her was better than she deserved.

The plane landed on a small airstrip on Crete. A car met them and whisked them away, past hotels and streets crowded with vacationers, to the docks where sleek yachts bobbed at anchor.

Laurel smiled tightly. Of course. That was a Greek tradition, wasn't it? If you were what Susie had called a zillionaire Adonis, you owned a ship and, yes, Damian led her to one—but it was not a yacht. The *Circe* was a sailboat, large, well kept and handsome, but as different from the huge yachts moored all around her as a racehorse is from a Percheron.

"Damian," a male voice cried.

A man appeared on deck, opening his arms as they climbed the gangplank toward him. He was short and wiry; he had a dark beard and a bald head and he wore jeans and a striped T-shirt, and though he bowed over Laurel's hand and made a speech she sensed was flowery even though she couldn't understand a word, he greeted Damian with a slap on the back and a hug hard enough to break bones.

Damian reciprocated. Then, grinning, the two men turned to Laurel.

"This is Cristos. He takes care of *Circe* for me, when I am away."

"How nice for you," Laurel said, trying to look bored. Not that it was easy. Somehow, she hadn't expected such relaxed give and take between the urbane Damian Skouras and this seaman.

Cristos said something. Damian laughed.

"He bids you welcome, and says to tell you that you are Aphrodite come to life."

"Really?" Laurel smiled coolly. "I thought it was Helen who was carried off against her will."

If she'd thought to rile Damian, she hadn't succeeded. He grinned, told her to stay put, clattered below deck and disappeared.

Stay, she thought irritably, as if she were a well-trained puppy.

Well, she wasn't well trained. And the sooner he understood that, the better for them both.

She rose from the seat where he'd placed her and started forward. Instantly Cristos was at her side. He smiled, said something that sounded like a question and stepped in front of her. Laurel smiled back.

"I'm just going to take a look around."

"Ah. No, madam. Sorry. Is not permitted."

So, he spoke English. And he had his orders. What did Damian think, that she was going to dive overboard and swim for her freedom?

Actually it wasn't a bad idea.

Laurel sighed, wrapped her hands around the railing and gazed blindly out to sea.

It was too late for that.

She was trapped.

She didn't recognize Damian, when he reappeared.

Was this man dressed in cutoff denims, a white T-shirt and sneakers her urbane husband? And why the change of clothing? It was hot, yes, and the sun beat down mercilessly, but surely it would be cooler, once they set sail.

But Damian's change of clothes had nothing to do with the climate. Every captain needed a crew, and Cristos's crew was Damian.

Except she had it backward. In seconds, she realized that Damian was in charge here, not just in name but in fact.

There was a subtle change that took place between the two men as soon as Damian came up the ladder. Even she could sense it, though the men worked together easily. Still, there was no question about who was the leader.

It was Damian, and he led not by command but by example.

She watched him as he took the boat through the narrow channel that led to the open sea. His dark, wind-tossed hair curled around his face. Sunlight glinted on the tiny stud in his ear and when the sun grew too hot, he pulled off his T-shirt and tossed it aside.

Laurel felt her breath catch. She'd blocked the memory of how he'd looked, naked, during the night they'd spent together. Now, she was confronted with his perfect masculinity. He was the elemental male, this stranger she'd married, strong, and powerful, and beautiful to see.

The breeze caught at her hair and whipped it free of the pins she'd carefully replaced during the drive from the airport. She put her hand up to catch the wild curls and suddenly Damian was there, beside her.

"Are you all right?"

Laurel nodded. He was so close to her that she could smell the sun and salt on his skin, and the musky aroma of his sweat. She imagined pressing her lips to his throat, tasting him with the tip of her tongue.

"Yes," she said, "yes, I'm fine."

His hand fell on her shoulder. "You'd tell me if you felt ill, wouldn't you?"

"Damian, really, I'm okay. The nausea is all gone, and you know that Dr. Glassman gave me a clean bill of health."

"And the name of a physician on Crete," he said, and smiled at Laurel's look of surprise. "I told her where I was taking you, and she approved."

He wouldn't have taken her on this trip otherwise. Still, out here on the sea, with the wind blowing and the waves rising to slap against the hull, he was struck again by his bride's fine-boned delicacy.

"Go on," she said, with a little smile that might almost have been real, "Sail your boat. I don't need watching."

His lips curved in a smile. He bent his head and put his lips to her ear, and she shuddered as she felt the soft warmth of his breath.

"Ah," he whispered, "you are wrong, my beautiful wife. Watching is exactly what you need, if a man is to feed his soul."

She tilted her head back and looked at him and when she did, he wrapped his hand around the back of her neck, bent his head and kissed her, hard, on the mouth.

"Leave your hair loose for me," he said, and then he kissed her again before scrambling lithely back to the helm.

Laurel waited until her heartbeat steadied, then raised her head and found Damian looking at her. This was the way a flower must feel, she thought dazedly, as its tightly closed petals unfurl beneath the kiss of the sun.

His final words whispered through her head. Leave your hair loose, he'd said, just like the night they'd made love, just before he'd undressed her, with such slow, sweet care that her heart had almost stopped beating.

But that night was far behind them, and it had no meaning.

Her shoulders stiffened. Defiantly she raised her arms and began to pin up her hair again.

And then the wind gusted, and before she could prevent it, the pins sailed from her hand and disappeared into the sea.

CHAPTER NINE

THE ISLAND ROSE before them an hour later.

"Actos," Damian said, coming up beside Laurel. She knew, from the way he said it that this was their destination.

She shaded her eyes with her hand and gazed over the narrowing strip of blue water that separated the *Circe* from a small, crescent-shaped harbor. No yachts bobbed at anchor here; the few boats moored were small, sturdy-looking fishing vessels. Square, whitewashed houses topped with red tile roofs stood clustered in the shadow of the sun-baked, rocky cliffs that rose behind them. Overhead, seabirds wheeled against the pale blue sky, their shrill cries echoing over the water.

All at once, Laurel thought of how she had wept last night, as she'd thought of the unknown days and years that lay ahead, and she shuddered.

Damian put his arm around her and drew her against his side.

"What is it? Are you ill?"

"No. No, I told you, I'm fine."

He stepped in front of her, leaned back against the rail of the boat and drew her between his legs. His body felt hard and hot, and the faint male smell of his skin rose to her nostrils. Another tremor went through her. This man was her husband.

Her husband.

"You *are* ill! You're as white as a sheet." His mouth twisted. "I should have realized. The motion of the boat…"

"Damian, really, I'm okay. It's just—too much sun,

127

maybe." She smiled brightly. "I'm used to the concrete canyons of New York, remember?"

"I wasn't thinking. We should have made this trip in two days instead of one." The wind ruffled her hair and he caught a strand of it in his fingers. It felt silky, and warm, and he fought to keep from bringing it to his lips. "I should have considered your condition when I made these plans."

His hand dropped to the curve of her shoulder and he stroked his thumb lightly against her neck. She had the sudden desire to close her eyes, lean into the gentle caress and give herself up to his touch.

The realization frightened her, and she gave herself up, instead, to a sharp response.

"You should have considered a lot of things, Damian, but you didn't, and here we are."

His hand fell away from her. "Yes," he said, "and here we are."

When Laurel had come to Greece before, it had been to do a cover for *Femme*. They'd shot it on a tiny island that had stunned her with its natural beauty.

Actos was not such a place.

If the island was beautiful, she was hard-pressed to see it. A rusted Ford station wagon was waiting for them at the dock, its mustachioed driver as ancient and gnarled as an olive tree. He and Damian greeted each other quietly, though she noticed that when they clasped hands, the men looked deep into each other's eyes and smiled.

The old man turned to her and took off his cap. He smiled, bowed and said something to Damian.

"Spiro says he is happy to meet you."

"Tell Spiro I am glad to meet him, too."

"He says you are more lovely than Aphrodite, and that I am a very fortunate man to have won you."

"Tell him Aphrodite's an overworked image but that I thank him anyway for being such a charming liar, and that you are not fortunate, you are a scheming tyrant who black-mailed me into marriage.''

Damian laughed. ''That would not upset Spiro. He still remembers the old days, when every man was a king who could as easily take a woman as ask for her.''

The old man leaned toward Damian and said something. Both men chuckled.

Laurel looked from one to the other. ''What did he say now?''

''He said that your eyes are cool.''

''It is more than my eyes that are cool, Damian. And I fail to see why that should make the two of you smile.''

''Because,'' he said, his smile tilting, ''Spiro tells me there is a saying in the village of his birth. A woman who is cold in the day fills the night with heat.''

A flush rose in her cheeks. ''It's amazing, how wrong an old saying can be.''

''Is it, my sweet wife?''

''Absolutely, my unwanted husband.''

Spiro muttered again and Laurel rolled her eyes.

''I feel like the straight man in a comedy act,'' she snapped. ''Now what?''

Damian moved closer to her. ''He thinks there is more than coolness in your eyes,'' he said softly. ''He says you do not look like a happy woman.''

''A clever man, this Spiro.''

''It is, he says, my responsibility to make you happy.''

''Did you tell him you could have done that by leaving me alone?''

Damian's slow smile was a warning, but it came too late. His fingers threaded in her hair and he bent his head and kissed her.

''Kissing me to impress the old man is pathetic,'' Laurel said, when he drew back. She spoke calmly and told herself that the erratic beat of her pulse was the result of weariness, and the sun.

Damian kissed her again, as gently as he had when she'd said 'No' at their wedding.''

"I kiss you because I want to kiss you," he said, very softly, and then he turned away and helped Spiro load their luggage into the old station wagon, while Laurel fought to still her racing heart.

A narrow dirt road wound its way up the cliffs, through groves of dark cypresses and between outcroppings of gray rock. They passed small houses that grew further and further apart as they climbed. After a while, there were no houses at all, only an occasional shepherd's hut. The heat was unrelenting, and a chorus of cicadas filled the air with sound.

The road grew even more narrow. Just when it seemed as if it would end among the clouds, a house came into view. It was made of white stone with a blue tile roof, and it stood on a rocky promontory overlooking the sea.

The house, and the setting, were starkly simple and wildly beautiful, and Laurel knew instantly that this was Damian's home.

A heavy silence, made more pronounced by the shrill of the cicadas and the distant pound of the surf, filled the car as Damian shut off the engine. Behind them, the car door creaked as Spiro got out. He spoke to Damian, who shook his head. The old man muttered in annoyance, doffed his cap to Laurel and set off briskly toward the house.

"What was that all about?"

Damian sighed. "He will be eighty-five soon, or perhaps even older. He's rather mysterious about his age." He got out of the car, came around to Laurel's door and opened it. "Still, he pretends he is a young man. He wanted to take our luggage to the house. I told him not to be such an old fool."

Laurel ignored Damian's outstretched hand and stepped onto the gravel driveway.

"So you told him to send someone else to get our things?"

Damian looked at her. "There is no one else at the house, except for Eleni."

"Eleni?"

"My housekeeper." He reached into the back of the wagon, picked up their suitcases and tossed them onto the grass, his muscles shifting and bunching under the thin cotton T-shirt. "Besides, why would I need anyone to do such a simple job as this?"

Her thoughts flashed back to Kirk, and the staff of ten who'd run his home. She'd never seen him carry anything heavier than his attaché case, and sometimes not even that.

"Well?" Damian's voice was rough. "What do you think? Can you survive a week alone with me, in this place?"

A week? Alone, here, with Damian? She didn't dare tell him what she really thought, that if he had set out to separate her from everything safe and familiar, he had succeeded.

"Well," she said coolly, "it's not Southampton. But I suppose there's hot water, and electricity, at least."

Out of the corner of her eye, she saw Damian's jaw tighten. Good, she thought with bitter satisfaction. What had he expected? Tears? Pleas? A fervent demand he take her somewhere civilized? If that was what he'd hoped for, he'd made an error. She wasn't going to beg, or grovel.

"I know it would please you if I said no." His smile was curt as he stepped past her, hoisted their suitcases and set off for the house. "But we have all the amenities you wish for, my dear wife. I know it spoils things for you, but I am not quite the savage you imagine."

The house was almost glacial, after the heat of the sun-baked hillside. White marble floors stretched to meet white painted walls. Ceiling fans whirred lazily overhead.

Damian dumped the suitcases on the floor and put his hands on his hips.

"Eleni," he roared.

A door slammed in the distance and a slender, middle-aged woman with eyes as dark as her hair came hurrying toward them. She was smiling broadly, but her smile vanished when she saw Damian's stern face. He said a few words to her, in Greek, and then he looked at Laurel.

"Eleni speaks no English, so don't waste your time trying to win her to your cause. She will show you to your room and tend to your needs."

The housekeeper, and not Damian. It was another small victory, Laurel thought, as he strode past her.

Eleni led the way up the stairs to a large, handsome bedroom with an adjoining bath.

Laurel nodded.

"Thank you," she said, "*efcharistó.*"

It was the only word of Greek she remembered from her prior trip. Eleni smiled her appreciation and Laurel smiled back at her, but when the door had shut and she was, at last, alone, her smile faded.

She had set out to irritate Damian and somehow, she'd ended up wounding him. It was more of a victory than she'd ever have hoped.

Why, then, did it feel so hollow?

The cypresses were casting long shadows over the hillside. Soon, it would be night.

Damian stood on the brick terrace and gazed at the sea. He knew he ought to feel exhausted. It had been a long day. An endless day, following hard on the heels of an endless week—a week that had begun with him thinking he'd never see Laurel again and ending with his taking her as his wife.

His wife.

His jaw knotted, and he lifted the glass of chilled *ouzo* to his lips and drank. The anise-flavored liquid slipped easily down his throat, one of the few pleasurable experiences in the entire damned day.

It still didn't seem possible. A little while ago, his life had been set on a fixed course with his business empire as its center. Now, in the blink of an eye, he had a wife, and a child on the way—a wife who treated him, and everything that was his, with such frigid distaste that it made his blood pressure rumble like the volcanos that were at the heart of these islands.

So she didn't like this house. Hell, why should she? He knew what it was, an isolated aerie on the edge of nowhere, and that he'd been less than forthright about its amenities, which began, and just about ended, with little more than electricity and hot water. She was a woman accustomed to luxury, and to the city. Her idea of paradise wasn't likely to include a house on top of a rocky hill overlooking the Aegean, where she was about to spend seven of the longest days of her life trapped with the fool who'd forced her into marriage.

Damian frowned and tossed back the rest of the *ouzo*.

What the hell had he been thinking, bringing her here? God knew this wasn't the setting for a honeymoon—not that this was going to be one. Spiro, that sly old fox, had slapped him on the back and said that it was about time he'd married. Damian had told him to mind his own business.

This wasn't a marriage, it was an arrangement...and maybe that was the best way to think about it. Marriage, under the best of circumstances, was never about love, not once you scratched the surface. It was about lust, or loneliness, or procreation. Well, in that sense, he and Laurel were ahead of the game. There was no pretense in their relationship, no pretending that anything but necessity had brought them to this point in the road.

Damian refilled his glass and took a sip. Viewed reasonably, he really had no cause to complain. Not about having a child, at least. The more he'd thought about it the past week, the more pleased he'd been at the prospect of fatherhood. He'd enjoyed raising Nicholas, but the boy had come into his life almost full-grown. There'd be a special pleasure in holding an infant in his arms, knowing that it carried his name and his genes, that it would be his to mold and nurture.

His mouth twisted in a wry smile. And, despite all the advances of modern science, you still needed a woman to have a baby. A wife, if you wanted to do it right, and as wives went, Laurel would be eminently suitable.

She was beautiful, bright and sophisticated. She'd spent her life rubbing elbows with the rich and famous; to some degree, she was one of them herself. She'd be at ease as the hostess of the parties and dinners his work demanded, and he had no doubt that she'd be a good mother to their child.

As for the rest…as for the rest, he thought, the heat pooling in his loins, what would happen between them in bed would keep them both satisfied. She would not deny him forever. She wouldn't want to. Despite her protestations, Laurel wanted him. She was a passionate woman with a taste for sex, but she was his now. If she ever thought to slake her thirst with another man, he'd—he'd…

The glass splintered in his hand. Damian hissed with pain as the shards fell to the terrace floor.

"Dammit to hell!"

Blood welled in his palm. He cursed again, dug in his pocket for a handkerchief—and just then, a small, cool hand closed around his.

"Let me see that," Laurel said.

He looked up, angry at himself for losing control, angry at her for catching him, and the breath caught in his throat.

How beautiful his wife was!

She was wearing something long, white and filmy; he thought of what Spiro had said, that she looked like Aphrodite, but the old man was wrong for surely the goddess had never been this lovely.

Laurel must have showered and washed her hair. It hung

loose in a wild cloud of dark auburn curls that tumbled over her shoulders as she bent over his cut hand.

"It isn't as bad as it probably feels," she said, dabbing at the wound with his handkerchief.

He felt a fist close around his heart. Yes, it was, he thought suddenly, it was every bit as bad, and maybe worse.

"Come inside and let me wash it."

He didn't want to move. The moment was too perfect. Laurel's body, brushing his. Her hair, tickling his palm. Her breath, warm on his fingers...

"Damian?" She looked up at him. "The cut should be— it should be..."

Why was he looking at her that way? His eyes were as dark as the night that waited on the rim of the sea. There was a tension in his face, in the set of his shoulders...

His wide shoulders, encased in a dark cotton shirt. She could see the golden column of his throat at the open neck of the shirt; the pulse beating in the hollow just below his Adam's apple; the shadow of dark, silky hair she knew covered his hard-muscled chest.

A chasm seemed to open before her, one that terrified her with its uncharted depth.

"This cut should be washed," she said briskly, "and disinfected."

"It is not necessary." His voice was low and throaty; it made her pulse quicken. "Laurel..."

"Really, Damian. You shouldn't ignore it."

"I agree. A thing like this must not be ignored."

Her eyes met his and a soft sound escaped her throat. "Damian," she whispered, "please..."

"What?" he said thickly. He lifted his uncut hand and pushed her hair back from her face. "What do you want of me, *kalí mou*? Tell me, and I will do it."

Kiss me, she thought, and touch me, and let me admit the truth to myself, that I don't hate you, don't despise you, that I—that I...

She let go of his hand and stepped back.

"I want you to let me clean this cut, and bandage it," she said briskly. "You've seen to it that we're a million miles from everything. If you developed an infection, I wouldn't even know how to get help."

Damian's mouth twisted.

"You are right." He wound the handkerchief around his hand and smiled politely. "You would be stranded, not just with an unwanted husband but with a disabled one. How selfish of me, Laurel. Please, serve yourself some lemonade. Eleni prepared it especially for you. I will tend to this cut, and then we shall have our dinner. You will excuse me?"

Laurel nodded. "Of course," she said, just as politely, and she turned and stared out over the sea, watching as a million stars fired the black velvet sky, and blinking back tears that had risen, inexplicably, in her eyes.

She woke early the next morning.

The same insect chorus was singing, accompanied now by the soaring alto of a songbird. It wasn't the same as awakening to an alarm clock, she thought with a smile, or to the honking of horns and the sound of Mr. Lieberman's footsteps overhead.

Dressed in a yellow sundress, she wandered through the house to the kitchen. Eleni greeted her with a smile, a cup of strong black coffee and a questioning lift of the eyebrows that seemed to be the equivalent of, "What would you like for breakfast?"

A bit of sign language, some miscommunication that resulted in shared laughter, and Laurel sat down at the marble-topped counter to a bowl of fresh yogurt and sliced strawberries. She ate hungrily—the doors leading out to the terrace were open, and the air, fragrant with the mingled scents of flowers and of the sea, had piqued her appetite. She poured herself a second cup of coffee and sipped it outdoors, on the terrace, and then she wandered down the steps and onto the grass.

It was strange, how a night's sleep and the clear light of morning changed things. Yesterday, the house had seemed disturbingly austere but now she could see that it blended perfectly with its surroundings. The location didn't seem as forbidding, either. There was something to be said for being on the very top of a mountain, with the world laid out before you.

Impulsively she kicked off her sandals and looped the straps over her fingers. Then she set off toward the rear of the house, where she could hear someone—Spiro, perhaps—beating something with what sounded like a hammer.

But it wasn't the old man. It was Damian, wearing denim cutoffs, leather work gloves, beat-up sneakers and absolutely nothing else. He was wielding what she assumed was a sledgehammer, swinging it over and over against a huge gray boulder.

His swings were rhythmic; his attention was completely focused on the boulder. She knew he had no idea she was there and a part of her whispered that it was wrong to stand in the shadow of a cypress and watch him this way...but nothing in the world could have made her turn away or take her eyes off her husband.

How magnificent he was! The sun blazed down on his naked shoulders; she could almost see his skin toasting to a darker gold as he worked. His body glistened under a fine layer of sweat that delineated its muscled power. He grunted softly each time he swung the hammer and she found herself catching her breath at each swing, holding it until he brought the hammer down to smash against the rock.

Her thoughts flashed two years back, to Kirk, and to the hours he'd spent working out in the elaborate gym in the basement of his Long Island home. Two hours a day, seven days a week, and he'd still not looked as beautifully male as Damian did right now.

She thought of how strong Damian's arms had felt

around her the night they'd made love, of how his muscles had rippled under her hands...

"Laurel."

She blinked. Damian had turned around. He smiled, put down the hammer and wiped his face and throat with a towel that had been lying in the grass.

"Sorry," he said, tossing the towel aside and coming toward her. "I didn't mean to wake you."

"You didn't. I've always been an early riser."

He stripped off his gloves and tucked them into a rear pocket.

"I am, too. It's an old habit. If you want to get any work done in the summer here, you have to start before the sun is too high in the sky or you end up broiled to a crisp. Did you sleep well?"

Laurel nodded. "Fine. And you?"

"I always sleep well, when I am home."

It was usually true, though not this time. He'd lain awake half the night, thinking about Laurel, lying in a bed just down the hall from his. When he'd finally dozed off, it was only to tumble into dreams that had left him feeling frustrated. He'd figured on working that off this morning through some honest sweat, but just the sight of his wife, standing like a barefoot Venus with the wind tugging at her hair and fluttering the hem of her sundress, had undone all his efforts.

Laurel cleared her throat. "What are you doing, anyway?"

"Being an idiot," he said, and grinned at her. "Or so Spiro says. I thought it would be nice to plant a flower garden here."

"And Spiro doesn't approve?"

"Oh, he approves. It's just that he's convinced that I will never defeat the boulder, no matter how I try." He bent down, picked up a handful of earth and let it drift through his fingers. "He's probably right but I'll be damned if I'll give in without a fight."

She couldn't imagine Damian giving in to anything without a fight. Wasn't that the reason she was here, as his wife?

"Besides, I've gotten soft lately."

He didn't look soft. He looked hard, and fit, and wonderful.

"Too many days behind a desk, too many fancy lunches." He smiled. "I can always find ways to work off a few pounds, when I come home to Actos."

"You grew up here, in this house?"

Damian laughed. "No, not quite. Here." He plucked her sandals from her hand and knelt down before her. "Let me help you with these."

"No," she said quickly, "that's all right. I can..." He lifted her foot, his fingers long and tan against the paleness of her skin. Her heart did another of those stutter-steps, the foolish ones that were coming more often, and for no good reason. "Damian, really." Irritation, not with him but with herself, put an edge on her words. "I'm not an invalid. I'm just—"

"Pregnant," he said softly, as he rose to his feet. His eyes met hers, and he put his hand gently on her flat stomach. "And with my child."

Their eyes met. It was hard to know which burned stronger, the flame in his eyes or the heat in his touch. Deep within her, something uncoiled lazily and seemed to slither through her blood.

"Come." He held out his hand.

"No, really, I didn't mean to disturb you. You've work to do."

"The boulder and I are old enemies. We'll call a truce, for now." He smiled and reached for her hand. "Come with me, Laurel. This is your home, too. Let me show it to you."

It wasn't; it never would be. She wanted to tell him that but he'd already entwined his fingers with hers and anyway, what harm could there be in letting him walk her around?

"All right," she said, and fell in beside him.

He showed her everything, and she could tell from the way he spoke that he took a special pride in it all. The old stone barns, the pastures, the white specks in a lower valley that he said were sheep, even the squawking chickens that fluttered out of their way…it all mattered to him, and she could see in the faces of the men who worked for him, tilling the land and caring for the animals, that they knew it, and respected him for it.

At last he led her over the grass, down a gentle slope and into a grove of trees that looked as if they'd been shaped by the wind blowing in from the sea.

"Here," he said softly, "is the true heart of Actos."

"Are these olive trees? Did you plant them?"

"No," he said, with a little smile, "I can't take any credit for the grove. The trees are very old. Hundreds of years old, some of them. I'm only their caretaker, though I admit that it took years to restore them to health. This property had been left unattended for a long time, before I bought it."

"It wasn't in your family, then?"

"You think this house, this land, was my inheritance?" He laughed, as if she'd made a wonderful joke. "Believe me, it was not." His smile twisted; he tucked his hands into his back pockets and looked at her, his gaze steady. "The only thing I inherited from my parents was my name—and sometimes, I even wonder about that."

"I'm sorry," Laurel said quickly. "I didn't mean to pry."

"No, don't apologize. You have the right to know these things about me." A muscled knotted in his jaw. "My father was a seaman. He made my mother pregnant, married her only because she threatened to go to the police with a tale of rape, and left her as soon as I was born."

"How terrible for her!"

"Don't waste your pity." He began walking and Laurel hurried to catch up. Ahead, a low stone wall rose marked the edge of the cliff, and the bright sea below. "I doubt it

happened as she described it. She was a tavern whore."
His voice was cold, without inflection; they reached the
wall and he leaned against it and stared out over the water.
"She told me as much, when she'd had too much to drink."

"Oh, Damian," Laurel said softly, "I'm so sorry."

"For what? It is reality, and I tell it to you not to elicit
your pity but only because you're entitled to know the
worst about the man you've married."

"And the best." She drew a deep breath and made the
acknowledgment she'd refused to make until this moment.
"Your decision about this baby—our baby—wasn't one
every man would choose."

"Still, it was not a decision to your liking."

"I don't like having my decisions made for me."

A faint smile curved over his mouth. "Are you suggest-
ing that I am sometimes overbearing?"

Laurel laughed. "Why do I suspect you've heard that
charge before?"

The wind lifted his dark hair and he brushed it back off
his forehead. It was a boyish gesture, one that suited his
quick smile.

"Ah, now I see how things are to be. You and Spiro
will combine forces to keep me humble."

"You? Humble?" She smiled. "Not unless that old man
is more of a miracle worker than I am. Who is he, anyhow?
I got the feeling he's more than someone who works for
you."

Damian leaned back, elbows on the wall, and smiled.

"What would you call a man who saves not only your
life, but your soul?" A breeze blew a curl across her lips.
He reached out and captured the strand, smoothing it gently
with his fingers. "Spiro found me, on the streets of Athens.
I was ten, and I'd been on my own for two years."

"But what happened to your mother?"

He shrugged. It was a careless gesture but it couldn't
mask the pain in his words.

"I woke up one morning, and she was gone. She left me

a note, and some money... It didn't matter. I had been living by my wits for a long time by then.''

"How?" Laurel said softly, while she tried to imagine what it must have been like to be ten, and wake up and find yourself alone in the world.

"Oh, it wasn't difficult. I was small, and quick. It was easy to swipe a handful of fruit or a couple of tomatoes from the outdoor markets, and a clever lad could always con the tourists out of a few drachma." The wind tugged at her hair again, and he smoothed it back from her cheek and smiled. "I was quite an accomplished little pickpocket, until one winter day when Spiro came into my life."

"You stole from him, and he caught you?"

Damian nodded. "He was old as Methuselah, even then, but strong as an olive tree. He gave me a choice. The po-lice—or I could go with him." He smiled. "I went with him."

"Damian, I'm lost here. Didn't you have a sister? Nicholas—the boy who married my niece—is your nephew, isn't he?"

"It's how his mother and I thought of each other, as brother and sister, but, in truth, we weren't related. You see, Spiro brought me here, to Actos, where he lived. The summer I was thirteen, an American couple—Greeks, but generations removed—came to the island, searching for their roots. Spiro decided I needed a better future than he could provide and, since I'd learned some English in Athens when I'd conned tourists, he convinced the Americans to take me to the States."

"And they agreed?"

"They were good people and Spiro played on all their Greek loyalties. They took me home with them, to New York, and enrolled me in school. I studied hard, won a scholarship to Yale..." He shrugged. "I was lucky."

"Lucky," she said softly, thinking of the boy he'd been and the man he'd become.

"Luck, hard work...who knows where one begins and

the other ends? The only certainty is that if it hadn't been for Spiro, I would be living a very different life.''

She smiled. ''I'll have to remember to thank him.''

''Will you?'' His dark, thick lashes drooped over his eyes, so that she couldn't quite see them. ''If he'd left me on the streets, I'd never have stormed into your life and turned it upside down.''

''I know.''

The words, said so softly that they were little more than a whisper, hung in the air between them. Damian framed Laurel's face in his hands. Her eyes gave nothing away, but he could see the sudden, urgent beat of her pulse in the hollow of her throat.

''*Mátya mou,*'' he whispered.

''What does that mean? *Mátya mou?*''

Damian bent his head and brushed his mouth gently over hers. ''It means, my dearest.''

She smiled tremulously. ''I like the sound of the words. Would it be difficult, to learn Greek?''

''I'll teach you.'' His thumb rubbed lightly over her bottom lip. ''I'll do whatever makes you happy, if you tell me what's in your heart.''

A lie would have been self-protective, but how could she lie to this man, who had just opened himself to her?

''I—I can't,'' she said. ''I don't know what's in my heart, Damian. I only know that when I'm with you, I feel—I feel...''

His mouth dropped to hers in a deep, passionate kiss. For one time-wrenching moment, Laurel resisted. Then she sighed her husband's name, put her arms around his neck and kissed him back.

CHAPTER TEN

LAUREL'S KISS almost undid him.

It was not so much the heated passion of it; it was the taste of surrender he drank from her lips.

She had been his, but only temporarily on that night in New York. Now, holding his wife in his arms on a wind-swept hill above the Aegean, Damian made a silent vow. This time, when he made love to her, she would be his forever.

Was he holding her too closely? Kissing her too hard? He knew he might be and he told himself to hold back—but he couldn't, not when Laurel's mouth was so soft and giving beneath his, not when he could feel her heart racing, and he knew that her desire burned as brightly as his. Desire, and something more.

He couldn't think. All he could do was feel, and savor, and when she moaned softly and pressed herself against him, so that he could feel her body molded to his, he almost went out of his head with need.

"Damian," she whispered. Her voice broke. "Damian, please..."

He thrust his hands into her hair, his thumbs tracing the delicate arch of her cheeks, and lifted her face to his. Her eyes were dark with desire; color stained her cheeks.

"Tell me," he murmured, just as he had that first time, and he moved against her so that she caught her breath at the feel of him. "Say it, *o kalí mou*."

Laurel brushed her lips against his. "Make love to me," she sighed, and he caught her up in his arms and carried her to a stone watchtower that was a part of the wall.

The tower was ancient, older, even, than the wall. A

thousand years before, it had been a place from which warriors safeguarded the island against pirates. Now, as Damian lay his wife down gently on a floor mounded with clean, sweet-smelling hay, he knew that the battle that would be fought here today was one in which there would be no way to tell who was the conqueror and who the conquered.

He told himself to undress her slowly, despite the hunger that beat within him. But when she moved her hands down his chest, down and down until she cupped his straining arousal, the last semblance of his control slipped away.

"Now," he said fiercely, and he tore away her sundress.

Beneath, she was all lace and silk, perfumed flesh and heat. He tried again to slow what was happening but Laurel wouldn't let him. She lifted her head, strained to kiss his mouth; she stroked his muscled shoulders and chest, drew her hand down his hard belly, and then her fingers slid under the waistband of his shorts. Damian groaned; his hands closed over hers and together, they stripped the shorts away.

At last, they lay skin against skin, heat against heat, alone together in the universe.

"Damian," Laurel said brokenly, and he bent his head to hers and kissed her.

"Yes, sweetheart, yes, *o kalóz mou*."

And then he was inside her, thrusting into the heart of her, and in that last instant before she shattered in her husband's arms, Laurel, at last, admitted the truth to herself.

She was in love, completely in love, with Damian Skouras.

A long time later, in the white-hot blaze of midday, they made their way to the house.

Someone—Eleni, probably—had closed the thin-slatted blinds at all the windows so that the foyer was shadowed and cool. Everything was silent, except for the soft drone of the fan blades rotating slowly overhead.

Laurel looked around warily. "Where's Eleni?"

"Why? Do you need something?" Damian pulled her close and kissed her, lingeringly, on the mouth. "Let me get whatever it is. I've no wish to share you with anyone else just now."

"I don't need anything, Damian. I was just thinking…" She blushed. "If she sees us, she'll know that we—that you and I—"

Damian smiled. Bits of hay were tangled in his wife's hair, and there was a glow to her skin that he knew came from the hours she'd spent in his arms.

"What will she know, *keería mou*, except that we have made love?"

"What does that mean? Keerya moo?"

"It means that you are my wife." He pressed a kiss into her hair. "And a husband may make love to his wife whenever he chooses." He put his hand under her chin and gently lifted her face to his. "On Actos, in New York…anywhere at all, so long as she is willing. Do you agree?"

"Only if the same rules apply for the wife."

Damian's eyes darkened. "Has no one ever told you that democracy was invented here, in these islands?"

Laurel smiled. "In that case…"

She rose on her toes, put her mouth to her husband's ear and whispered.

Damian laughed. "I couldn't have put it better myself," he said, and he lifted her into his arms, carried her up the stairs and into his bedroom.

The days, and the nights, flew past. And each was a revelation.

Damian, the man who could do anything from saving a dying corporation to making an endless assault against a boulder, turned out to have a failing.

A grave one, Laurel said, with a solemnity she almost managed to pull off.

He didn't know how to play gin rummy.

He was, he assured her, an expert at baccarat and chemin de fer, and he admitted he'd even been known to win a dollar or two at a game of poker.

Laurel wasn't impressed. How could he have reached the age of forty without knowing how to play gin?

"Thirty-eight," he said, with only a glint in his eye, and then he said, well, if she really wanted to teach him the game, he supposed he'd let her.

He lost six hands out of six.

"I don't know," he said, with a sigh. "Gin just doesn't seem terribly interesting."

"Well, we could try playing for points. I'll keep score, or I can show you...what's the matter?"

"Nothing. It's just... I don't know. Points, scoring...it seems dull."

"Okay, how about playing for money?"

"A bet, you mean? Yes, that would be better."

"A nickel a hand."

Damian's brows lifted. "You call that interesting?"

"Maybe I should tell you that I'm the unofficial behind-the-runways-from-Milan-to-Paris gin rummy champion."

"So? What's the matter? Afraid of losing your title?"

Laurel blew her hair back out of her eyes. "Okay, killer, don't say I didn't warn you. We'll play big time. A dime a hand."

Damian's smile was slow and sexy. "I've got a better idea. Why don't we play for an article of clothing a hand?"

Laurel's eyes narrowed. "You sure you never played gin before?"

"Never," he said solemnly, and dealt out the cards.

Half an hour later, Laurel was down to a pair of jeans and a silk teddy. Her sandals, belt, shirt, even the ribbon she'd used to tie back her hair, lay on the white living-room carpet.

"No fair," she grumbled. "You *have* played gin before."

Damian gave her a heart-stopping smile and fanned out another winning hand. He leaned back against the cushions they'd tossed on the floor and folded his arms across his chest. "Well?"

Laurel smiled primly and took off an earring.

"Since when is an earring an article of clothing, *keería mou*? An article of clothing for each losing hand, remember?"

Her heart gave a little kick. "You wouldn't really expect me to—"

He reached out a lazy hand, drew his fingertip lightly over her breasts, then down to the waistband of her jeans. "Your game and your rules," he said huskily. "Take something off, sweetheart."

Laurel's eyes met his. She rose to her feet, undid the jeans and slid them off.

"Your turn is coming," she said, "just you wait and see."

He smiled and dealt the cards. It pleased her to see that his hands were unsteady. Surely he would lose now.

"Gin."

Laurel ran the tip of her tongue over her lips, and Damian's eyes followed the gesture. Heat began pooling in her belly.

"Damian, you're not going to make me..."

Their eyes met again. She swallowed dryly, then got to her knees. Slowly she hooked a finger under one shoulder strap and slid it off. She slid off the second. There were three satin ties on the teddy, just between her breasts, and she reached for them.

Damian's breathing quickened, but his eyes never left hers.

"One," she said softly. "Two. Three..."

With a throaty growl, he tumbled her to the carpet. And then, for a long, long time, the only sounds in the room were the sighs and whispers of love.

* * *

He refused to believe that she could cook.

They discussed it, one afternoon, as Laurel sat in a field of daisies with Damian's head in her lap.

She reminded him, indignantly, of the bread he'd found rising in her kitchen. He reminded her, not very gallantly, that it had resembled a science experiment gone bad.

Laurel plucked a handful of daisies and scattered them over his chest.

"I'll have you know that I make the most terrific sour-dough bread in the world."

"Uh-huh."

"What do you mean, 'uh huh'? I do. Ask George. He loves my bread."

"George," Damian scoffed. "The man's besotted. He'd say it was great even if it tasted like wet cardboard."

Laurel dumped more daisies over him. "He is not besotted with anyone but his own wife."

Damian sat up, reached for her hand and laced his fingers through hers. There was something he had to tell her, something he should have told her sooner. It meant nothing to him, but she had the right to know.

"It's good, for a man to be besotted with his wife," he said softly.

She smiled and brushed a daisy petal from his hair.

"Is it?"

"Did I ever tell you," he asked, catching her hand and raising it to his mouth, "that I was married before?"

Laurel's teasing smile vanished. "No. No, you didn't."

"Well, I was. For a grand total of three weeks."

"What happened?" She tried another smile and hoped this one worked. "Don't tell me. The lady served you a slice of wet cardboard, called it sourdough bread and you sent her packing."

"Nothing so simple. It turned out we had nothing in common. She wanted my name and my money, and I..."

"And you? What did you want?"

"Out," he said, with a little laugh, "almost from the

beginning. The marriage was a complete mistake. I think we both knew it."

"Why did you marry her, then?" A chill crept into Laurel's heart, and she gave him a stiff smile. "Was she pregnant, too?"

She regretted the ugly words as soon as she'd said them, but it was too late to call them back. Damian sat up, his face cold and hard.

"No. She was not pregnant. Had she been, I can assure you, I would still be married to her."

"Because it would have been your duty." Laurel stood up and dusted the grass from her shorts. "Of course," she said, and started briskly toward the house, "I almost forgot how noble you are, Damian. Sorry."

"*Theé mou!*" Angrily he clasped her shoulders and spun her around. "What is the matter with you, Laurel? Are you angry with me for having divorced a woman I did not love? Or for admitting that I would have done the right thing by her, if I'd had to?"

"I'm not angry with you at all." Her smile was brittle. "I'm just—you can't blame me for being curious, Damian. After all, I only just found out you have an ex-wife."

"I told you, the relationship was meaningless. We met, we thought we were in love, we got married. By the time we realized what we'd done, it was too late."

"Yes, well, that's what happens, when a person marries impetuously."

"Dammit, don't give me that look!"

"What look? It's the only one I've got—but how would you know that?"

"Don't be a little fool!" Damian glared at her, his face dark with anger. "There is no comparison between this marriage and the other. I married you because—because..."

"Because I was pregnant."

"Yes. No. I mean..." What did he mean? Of course he'd married her because she was pregnant; why deny it? What other reason could possibly have made him ask Laurel to be his wife?

"You needn't explain." Laurel's voice was frosty, a perfect match to her smile. "We both know what an honorable man you are. You married me for the sake of our child, and you'll stay married to me for the same reason. Isn't that right?"

Damian's jaw knotted. "You're damned right," he growled. "I'm going to stay married to you, and you to me, until as the man said, 'Death do us part.'"

He pulled her into his arms and kissed her just as he had the day he'd announced he was going to make her his wife. For the first time since they'd made love in the tower overlooking the sea, Laurel didn't respond. She felt nothing, not desire, not even anger.

"You are my wife," Damian said. Stone-faced, he held her at arm's length and looked down into her face. "And nothing more needs to be said about it."

Laurel wrenched free of his grasp. "How could I possibly forget that, when you'll always be there to remind me?"

She swung away and strode up the hill, toward the house. Damian's hands knotted at his sides. Dammit, what was wrong with her? He thought they'd gotten past this, that Laurel had made peace with the circumstances of their marriage, but it was clear that she hadn't.

Had she been pretending, all those times they'd made love? Had she lain in his arms, touching him, kissing him, and wishing all the while that he'd never forced her into becoming his wife? Because he had. Hell, there was no denying it. He'd given her about as much choice in the matter as the rocks below gave to the ships they'd claimed, over the centuries.

His mouth twisted. So what? They were man and wife. She had to accept that. As for this afternoon's pointless quarrel...she'd get over it when he took her to bed, tonight.

He took a deep breath, stuck his hands into his pockets and stood staring out to sea.

She hadn't been pretending, when they made love. He would have known if those sweet sighs, those exciting whispers, had been false.

Of course, he would... Wouldn't he?

Laurel sat at the dressing table in the bedroom where she'd spent her first night as Mrs. Damian Skouras, staring at her reflection in the mirror.

She hadn't been back in this room since then. Every night—and a lot of long, wonderful mornings and afternoons—had been spent in Damian's bed.

Her hand trembled as she picked up a silver-backed brush and ran it over her hair.

What had gotten into her today? Damian had been married before. Well, so what? She'd had a relationship before, too, and even if Kirk hadn't treated it as a marriage, she had. She'd been faithful, and loving, and when she'd found out that he'd deceived her, her heart couldn't have been more broken than if she had been Mrs. Kirk Soames. She'd loved Kirk every bit as much as if—as if—

A choked cry burst from her lips and she dropped the brush and buried her face in her hands.

It wasn't true. She'd never really loved Kirk, she knew that now. What she felt for Damian made her feelings for Kirk seem insignificant.

And that was what this afternoon's performance had been all about, wasn't it?

"Wasn't it?" she whispered, lifting her head and staring at her pale face and tear-swollen eyes in the mirror.

Damian had told her he'd been married before, that it had been an impetuous marriage and hadn't worked out, and all she'd been able to think was that he'd married her the same way, impetuously, because it had been the right thing to do.

How she'd longed for him to deny it!

I married you because I love you, she'd wanted him to say, because I'll always love you.

But he hadn't. He'd married her because he wanted his child to have a father, and even though part of her knew how right, how decent, that was, another part of her longed to hear him say he'd married her for love.

She picked up the hairbrush again and stared at her reflection.

But he hadn't. She was Damian's wife, but not his love. She had his name, and his interest in bed, but if she made many more scenes like the one she'd made today, she probably wouldn't even have that, and never mind the Until death do us part promise. Her mouth turned down with bitterness. She knew all about men like Damian, and promises of fidelity. Oh, yes, she knew all about—

"Laurel?"

Her gaze flew to the mirror just as the bedroom door opened. Damian stood in the doorway, wearing a terry cloth robe. She knew from the experience of the past week that he had nothing on beneath it. His hair was tousled, his eyes were dark and she wanted nothing so much as to jump up and hurl herself into his arms.

Pride and pain kept her rooted in place.

"Yes, Damian," she said. She smiled politely, put down the brush and turned around.

"Are you feeling better?"

She'd missed dinner, pleading a headache. It would never have done to have told him the truth, that what ached was her heart.

"Much better, thank you. Eleni brought me some tea, and aspirin."

He nodded and stepped further into the room. "It's late."

"Is it? I hadn't noticed."

He paused beside her and lifted his hand. She thought, for a moment, he was going to touch her hair and if he had, that would have been her undoing. She'd have sighed under his hand like a kitten—but he didn't. He only reached out, straightened the dressing table mirror, then put his hand into his pocket.

"Are you coming to bed?"

Laurel turned away and looked into the mirror again. He'd asked the question so casually but then, why wouldn't he? So far as he was concerned, her place was in his bed. Not only was she his wife, but she'd made it clear she wanted to be there. Her throat constricted as she remembered the things they'd done together in that bed.

Why was it that loving a man who didn't love you, knowing he'd *never* love you, could suddenly make those things seem cheap?

"Actually," she said, picking up the brush again, "I thought I'd sleep in here tonight."

"In here?" he repeated, as if she'd suggested she was going to spend the night on an ice floe in the North Sea.

"Yes." Briskly, she drew the brush through her hair. "I still have a bit of a headache."

"Shall I phone the doctor Glassman recommended on Crete?"

"No. No, I don't need a doctor."

"Are you sure? Laurel, if you're ill—"

"I'm fine. The baby's fine." She smiled tightly at him in the mirror. "It's just an old habit of mine, Damian. Sometimes, I need a night to myself. Kirk used to say—"

"Kirk?" he said, and the way he said it made her heart stop.

Don't, she told herself, oh, don't do this...

"A man I used to live with. Well, actually, a man I thought about marrying. Didn't I ever tell you about him?"

"No," he said coldly, "you did not."

She looked into the mirror again and what she saw in his face terrified her. The brush clattered to the mirrored top of the dressing table and she swung toward him.

"Damian," she said quickly, but it was too late. He was already at the door.

"You're right," he said, "a night apart might be an excellent idea for the both of us. I'll see you in the morning."

"Damian, wait…"

Wait? He stepped into the hall and slammed the door after him. She wouldn't want him to wait, if she knew how close he was to smashing his fist into the wall. He stormed into his bedroom, kicked the door shut, then flung open the french doors that let out onto the terrace. The black heat of the Agean night curled around him like a choking fog.

All right, so she'd lived with a man. So what? It didn't matter a damn. She'd married him, not Kirk, whoever in hell Kirk might be.

Married him under protest. Under the threat of losing her child to him. Under the worst kind of blackmail.

Damian spun around and slammed his fist against the wall. It hurt like hell, and he winced and put his knuckles to his mouth, tasted the faint tang of blood, and wished to God it was Kirk's blood instead of only his own. What sort of name was that, anyway? A stupid name, befitting a man foolish enough to have let Laurel go.

Any man would want her. Would desire her. Would fall in love with her.

And, just that simply, Damian saw the truth.

He loved Laurel. He loved his wife.

"I love her," he said to the night, and then he laughed out loud.

What a fool he'd been, not to realize it sooner.

And maybe, just maybe, she loved him, too.

He lifted his face to the moonless sky, as if the answer might be there, in the blazing light of a million stars that dotted the heavens.

It would explain so much, if she did.

The softness of her, in his arms. The passion she could never hide when he touched her. Even her reaction earlier today, when he'd so clumsily told her that he'd been married before.

His heart filled with hope. Maybe what had seemed like

anger had really been pain. Maybe she'd felt the same jeal-
ousy at his mention of a former lover that he'd felt at the
mention of Kirk.

But if she loved him, would she have chosen to sleep
alone tonight? Would she have taken such relish in telling
him she'd lived with another man and almost married him?

Damian took a deep breath. He'd always prided himself
on knowing how to chart a direct path from A to B, but
tonight he felt as if he were going in circles.

There was only one thing to do, by God, go back into
Laurel's room, confront her, drag her from that bed if he
had to, shake her silly or kiss her senseless until she told
him what she felt for him...

The telephone rang. Damian cursed and snatched it up.

"Whoever you are," he snapped, "you'd better have a
damned good reason for calling."

It was Hastings, his personal attorney, phoning from
New York.

Damian sat down on the edge of the bed. Hastings was
not a man given to running the risk of waking his most
important client in the middle of the night.

"I'm afraid we have a problem, Mr. Skouras."

Damian listened and, as he did, the look on his face went
from dark to thunderous.

"Gabriella is suing me for breach of promise? Is she
crazy? She hasn't got a case. What do you mean, she's
going to sell her story to 'The Gossip Line' unless I meet
her demands? Who'd give a crap about...? What's my marriage got to do with...?" His face went white. "If she drags
my wife down into the mud, so help me God, I'll—"

Hastings spoke again. According to Gabriella, Damian
had made promises. He'd said he'd marry her. He'd been
not just her only lover but her first lover, since her divorce,
and her last.

Damian took a stranglehold on the telephone cord. "All
right," he said abruptly, rising to his feet and shrugging
off his robe. "Here's what I want you to do." He rattled

off a string of commands. Hastings repeated them, then asked a question, and Damian glared at the phone as if he could see the attorney's face in it. "How the hell do I know who to contact? That's why you're on retainer, Hastings, because you're the legal eagle, remember? Just get the information by tomorrow. That's right, man. Tomorrow. I'll see you in New York."

Rage and determination propelled him through the next few minutes. He phoned Spiro on the intercom, called his pilot on Crete—and then he hesitated.

Should he wake Laurel, to tell her he was leaving? No. Hell, no. The last thing he needed right now was to explain to his wife that his vindictive former mistress was trying to stir up trouble by selling a story to some TV gossip show featuring herself as an abandoned lover—and Laurel as a scheming, pregnant fortune hunter.

Spiro could deal with it. The old man could tell her he'd been called to New York on urgent business. She wouldn't like it, but how long would he be gone? A day? Two, at the most. Then he'd be back, on Actos, and he'd take his wife in his arms, tell her he loved her and pray to the gods that she would say she loved him, too. And if she didn't— if she didn't, he'd make her love him, dammit, he'd kiss her mouth until all memory of Kirk whoever-he-was had been wiped from her mind and her soul, and then they'd begin their lives together, all over again.

He just had to see her once, before he left. The house was quiet, as he left his room; no light spilled from beneath Laurel's closed door. Damian opened it and slipped inside.

She lay on her back, fast asleep.

How lovely she was. And how he adored her.

"*Kalí mou*," he murmured, "my beloved."

He bent and brushed his mouth gently over hers. She stirred and breathed a soft sigh, and it was all he could do to keep from lying down beside her and gathering her into his arms.

First, though, there was Gabriella to deal with.

Damian's jaw hardened as he left his wife's room and quietly shut the door after him.

And deal with the bitch, he would.

CHAPTER ELEVEN

LAUREL AWAKENED to bright sunlight and a memory as ethereal as a wisp of cloud.

Was it a dream, or had Damian really entered her room in the middle of the night, kissed her and called her his beloved?

It seemed so real...but it couldn't have been. They'd quarreled, and even though he'd held out a tentative olive branch, she'd rejected it.

She sat up, pushed aside the light sheet that covered her and scrubbed her hands over her face.

Rejected his peace offering? That was putting it mildly. She'd damn near slapped his face, then rubbed his nose in her relationship with Kirk for good measure.

Laurel puffed out her breath. What on earth had possessed her? The man she loved—the only man she'd ever loved—was Damian.

She dressed quickly, with little care for how she looked. All that mattered was finding a way to rectify the damage she'd caused last night. Damian didn't love her, not yet, but she knew that he cared for her—at least, he had, until she'd instigated that ugly scene.

Well, there was only one way to fix things.

She had to tell Damian the truth. To hell with pride, and the pain that would come of admitting she loved him without hearing that he loved her, too. She'd go to him, tell him that Kirk had never meant a damn to her, that no one had or ever would, except him.

Her heart was racing, as much with apprehension as with anticipation. After Kirk, she'd promised she'd never leave herself so vulnerable to any man again. But Damian wasn't *any* man. He was her husband, her lover—he was the man she would always love.

Laurel squared her shoulders and stepped out into the hall.

He wasn't in his bedroom. Well, why would he be? It was past eight o'clock, late by his standards, and there'd been nothing to make him linger in bed today. She hadn't been lying in the curve of his arm, her head pillowed on his shoulder; he hadn't whispered a soft, sexy "good morning" and she hadn't given him a slow, equally sexy smile in return.

He wasn't in the kitchen, either, nor on the terrace, sipping a second cup of coffee while he and Spiro conferred on what might need doing today.

Eleni was there, though, out on the terrace, busily watering the urns filled with pansies and fuchsias and impatiens.

"*Kaliméra sas.*"

Laurel smiled as she stepped outside. "*Kaliméra sas*, Eleni. Where is Mr. Skouras, do you know?"

Eleni's brows lifted. "Madam?"

"My husband," Laurel said. "Have you any idea where..." She sighed, smiled and shook her head. "Never mind. I'll find him, I'm sure."

But she didn't. He wasn't at the barns, or strolling along the wall, or hammering at the boulder.

"*Kaliméra sas.*"

It was Spiro. He had come up behind her, as quietly as a shadow.

"*Kaliméra sas*," Laurel said, and hesitated. The old man spoke no English and she spoke no Greek beyond the few words she'd picked up during the week. Still, it was worth a try. Damian had to be here somewhere. "Spiro, do you know where Mr. Skouras is?"

The old man's bushy brows lifted questioningly.

"I'm trying to find Damian. Damian," she repeated,

pointing at the platinum wedding band on her left hand, "you know, my husband."

"Ah. Damian. *Né*. Yes, I understand."

"You *do* speak English, then?"

"A little bit only."

"Believe me, your English is a thousand times better than my Greek. So, where is he?"

"Madam?"

"Damian, Spiro. Where is he?"

The old man cleared his throat. "He leave island, madam."

"Left Actos? For Crete, you mean?"

"He is for New York."

Laurel stared at him. "What do you mean, he's... No, Spiro, you must be mistaken. He wouldn't have gone to New York without me."

"He is for New York, madam. Business."

"Business," she repeated and then, without warning, she began to weep. She cried without sound, which somehow only made her tears all the more agonizing for Spiro to watch.

"Madam," he said unhappily, "please, do not cry."

"It's my fault," she whispered. "It's all my fault. We quarreled, and I hurt him terribly, and—and I never told him—he doesn't know how much I—"

She sank down on a bench and buried her face in her hands. Spiro stood over her, watching, feeling the same helplessness he'd felt years ago, when he'd come across a lamb who'd gotten itself caught on a wire fence.

He put out his hand, as if to touch her head, then reached into his pocket instead, pulled out an enormous white handkerchief, and shoved it into her hands.

"Madam," he said, "you will see. All will be well."

"No." Laurel blew her nose, hard, and rose to her feet. "No, it won't be. You don't understand, Spiro. I told Damian a lie. An awful lie. I said cruel things..."

"You love him," the old man said gently.

"Yes. Oh, yes, I love him with all my heart. If only I'd gone to him last night. If only I hadn't been so damn proud. If only I could go to him now…"

Spiro nodded. It was as he'd thought. Something had gone wrong between Damian and his bride; it was why he had left her in the middle of the night.

"Where are you going at such an hour?" Spiro had asked.

Damian's reply had been sharp. "New York," he'd said, "and before you ask, old man, no, Laurel does not know I'm going, and no, I am not going to tell her."

"But what shall I tell her, when she asks?"

"Tell her whatever seems appropriate," Damian had said impatiently, and then he'd motioned Spiro to cast off the line.

The old man frowned. Damian and this woman loved each other deeply, any fool could see that, but for reasons that were beyond him to comprehend, they could not admit it.

"Spiro."

He looked at the woman standing beside him. Her eyes were clear now, and fierce with determination.

"I know that you love Damian," she said. "Well, I love him, too. I have to tell him that, Spiro, I have to make him understand that there's never been anyone but him, that there never could be."

Tell her whatever seems appropriate…

The old man straightened his shoulders. "Yes," he said. He put his gnarled hand on Laurel's shoulder. "Yes, madam. You must tell him—and I will help you to do it."

New York City was baking in brutal, midsummer heat.

It had been hot on Actos, too, but there the bright yellow sun, blue sea and pale sky had given a strange beauty to the land.

Here, in Manhattan, the sun was obscured by a sullen sky. The air was thick and unpleasant. And, Damian thought as the doors of the penthouse elevator whispered open, it had been one hell of a long day.

He stripped off his jacket and tie, dumped them on a chair and turned up the air conditioner. A current of coolness hissed gently into the silent foyer. Stevens and his housekeeper were both on vacation; he had the place to himself. And that was just as well.

Damian closed his eyes and let the chill envelope him as he undid the top buttons of his shirt, then rolled back his cuffs. He was in no mood to pretend civility tonight, not after dealing with Gabriella. The hour he'd spent closeted with her and their attorneys had felt like an eternity. Even the cloying stink of her perfume was still in his nostrils.

"Are you certain you're up to a face-to-face meeting?" Hastings had asked him.

Damian had felt more up to putting his hands around Gabriella's throat, but he'd known this was the only thing that would work. She had to be confronted with the information he'd ordered gathered but, more than that, she had to see for herself that he would follow through.

For the next sixty minutes, while Gabriella wept crocodile tears into her lace handkerchief and cast him tragic looks, he'd tried to figure out what he'd ever imagined he'd seen in her.

The bleached hair. The artful but heavy makeup. The clinking jewelry—jewelry he'd paid for, from what he could tell—all of it offended him. The sole thing that kept him calm was the picture he held in his mind, of Laurel as he'd last seen her, asleep at Actos, in all her soft, unselfconscious beauty.

Finally he'd grown weary of the legal back-and-forth, and of Gabriella's posturing.

"Enough," he'd said.

All eyes had turned to him. In a voice that bore the chill of winter, he'd told Gabriella what she faced if she took him on and then, almost as an afterthought, he'd shoved the file folder across the conference table toward her.

"What is this, darling?" she'd said.

For the first time, he'd smiled. "Your past, *darling*, catching up to you."

She'd paled, opened the folder...and it was all over. Gabriella had called him names, many that were quite inventive; she'd hurled threats, too, but when her attorney peered over her shoulder at the contents of the folder, the list of names of the men she'd been involved with, the photos culled from the files of several private investigators including one of her, topless, sitting between the thighs of a naked man on a palm tree lined beach, he'd blanched and walked out.

Damian smiled, went to the bar and poured himself a shot of vodka over a couple of ice cubes.

"To private investigators," he said softly, and tossed back half his drink.

Glass in hand, he made his way up the stairs to his bedroom, the room where he'd first made love to his wife. And it *had* been love; he knew that now. It was illogical, it was almost embarrassingly romantic, but there wasn't a doubt in his mind that he'd fallen in love with Laurel at first sight.

He couldn't wait to tell her that.

As soon as he got back to Actos, he was going to take her in his arms and tell her what had been in his heart all the time, that he loved her and would always love her, that it didn't matter what faceless man she'd loved in the past because he, Damian Skouras, was her future, and the future was all that mattered.

He put down his drink, stripped off the rest of his clothes and stepped into the bathroom. His plane was waiting at the airport. Just another few hours, and he'd be home.

He showered quickly. There wasn't a minute to waste. The sooner he left here, the sooner he'd be in Laurel's arms.

But there was one stop to make first.

He knotted a bath sheet around his waist, ran his fingers

carelessly through his damp hair and retrieved his drink from the bedroom.

He was going to go to Tiffany's. He'd never given his wife an engagement ring. Well, he was going to remedy that failing right away. What would suit her best? Diamonds and emeralds? Diamonds and sapphires? Hell, maybe he'd solve the problem by buying her a whole bucketful of rings.

He grinned as he headed down the stairs. Another drink—ginger ale, because he wanted a clear head for this—and then he'd phone Tiffany's, see if they were open. If they weren't...what was the name of that guy he'd met last year? He was a Tiffany Veep, or maybe he was with Cartier or Harry Winston. Damian laughed out loud as he set his glass down on the bar. It didn't matter. Laurel wouldn't care where the ring was from, she wouldn't give a damn if it came from Sear's, not if she loved him, and he was closer and closer to being damned sure that she—

What was that?

Damian frowned. He could hear the soft hum of the elevator, see the lighted panel blinking as the car rose.

What the hell? He certainly wasn't expecting anyone, and the doorman would not send someone up without...

Unless it was Laurel.

His heart thudded.

That was impossible. She was on Actos. Or was she? Spiro hadn't approved of his hasty departure. In the old days, the old man had never hesitated to do what he thought best, even if it meant overriding Damian's wishes. Of course, a lot of years had gone by since then.

On the other hand, Spiro could still be stubborn. If he thought it wise to take matters into his own hands...

The elevator stopped, and Damian held his breath. The doors opened—and Gabriella stepped out of the car.

"Surprise," she said in a smoky contralto.

The sight of her, draped in hot pink that left nothing to the imagination and with a crimson smile painted on her lips, twisted his gut with such savage rage that it left him mute for long seconds. Then he drew a deep, painful breath and managed to find his voice.

"I'm not going to bother asking how you talked your way past the doorman," he said carefully. "I'm just going to tell you to turn around, get back into that elevator and get the hell out."

"Damian, darling, what sort of greeting is that?" Gabriella smiled and strolled past him, to the bar. "What are you drinking, hmm? Vodka rocks, it looks like. Well, I'll just have a tiny one, to keep you company."

"Did you hear me? Get out."

"Now, darling, let's not be hasty." She lifted her glass, took a sip, then put it down. "I know you were upset this morning, but it's my fault. I shouldn't have tried to convince you to come back to me the way I did."

"Convince me to…?" Damian put his fists on his hips. "Let's not play games, okay? What you tried was blackmail, and it didn't work. Now, do us both a favor and get out of here before it gets nasty."

Gabriella licked her lips. "Damian," she purred, "look, I understand. You married this woman. Well, you had no choice, did you? I mean, the word is out, darling, that your little Laurel got herself pregnant."

He came toward her so quickly that she stumbled backward. "I'll give you to the count of five," he snarled, "and then I'm going to take you by the scruff of your neck and toss you out the door. One. Two. Three…"

"Dammit," she said shrilly, "you cannot treat me like this! You made promises."

"You're a liar," he said flatly. "The only promise you've ever heard from me is this one. Go through that door on your own, or so help me…"

"Don't be a fool, Damian. You'll tire of her soon enough." Gabriella's hand went to the sash at her waist and pulled it. The hot pink silk fell open, revealing her naked body. "You'll want this. You'll want me."

Later, Damian would wonder why he hadn't heard the elevator as it made its return trip but then, how could he have heard anything, with each thud of his heart beating such dark fury through his blood?

"Cover yourself," he said, with disgust—and then he heard the sound of the elevator doors opening.

He saw Gabriella's quick, delighted smile and somehow, he knew, God, he knew...

He spun around and there was Laurel, standing in the open doors of the elevator.

"Laurel," he said, and when he started toward her, she threw up her hands and the look in her face went from shock to bone-deep pain.

"No," she whispered, and before he could reach her, she stabbed the button and the doors closed in his face.

And Damian knew, in that instant, that his last chance, his only chance, at love and happiness was gone from his life, forever.

CHAPTER TWELVE

RAIN POUNDED at the windows; late summer lightning split the low, gray sky as thunder rolled across the city.

Inside Laurel's kitchen, three women sat around the table. Two of them—Susie and Annie—were trying to look anywhere but at each other; the third—Laurel—was too busy glaring at her cup of decaf to notice.

"I *hate* decaffeinated coffee," Laurel said. "What is the point of drinking coffee if you're going to take out all the caffeine?"

Susie's gaze connected with Annie's. "Here we go again," her eyes said.

"It's better for you," she said mildly. "With the baby and all."

"I know that. For heaven's sakes, I'm the one who decided to give up coffee, aren't I? It's just that it's stupid to drink stuff that smells like coffee, looks like coffee, but tastes like—"

"Okay," Annie said, getting to her feet. She smiled brightly, whisked the coffee out from under Laurel's nose and dumped it into the sink. "Let's see..." She opened the cabinet and peered inside. "You've got a choice of herbal tea, cocoa, regular tea—"

"Regular tea's got as much caffeine as coffee. A big help you are, Annie."

Annie's brows shot skyward. "Right," she said briskly. She shut the cabinet and opened the refrigerator. "How about a nice glass of milk?"

"Yuck."

"Well, then, there's ginger ale. Orange juice." Her voice

grew muffled as she leaned into the fridge. "There's even a little jar of something that might be tomato juice."

"It isn't."

"V8?"

"No."

"Well, then, maybe it's spaghetti sauce."

"I don't remember the last time I had pasta."

Annie frowned and plucked the jar from the shelf. "It's not a good idea to keep chemistry experiments in the—"

Laurel shot to her feet. "Why did you say that?"

"Say what?" Annie and Susie exchanged another look. "Laurel, honey, if you'd just—"

"Just because a person finds something strange in another person's kitchen is no reason to say it looks like a— it looks like a..." Laurel took a deep breath. "Sorry," she said brightly. She looked from her big sister to her best friend. "Well," she said, in that same phony voice, "I know the two of you have things to do, so—"

"Not me," Susie said quickly. "George is downstairs, glued to the TV. I'm free as a bird."

"Not me, either," Annie said. "You know how it is. My life is dull, dull, dull."

"Dull? With your ex hovering in the background?" Laurel eyed her sister. "What's that all about, anyway? You're not seriously thinking of going down that road again, are you?"

For one wild minute, Annie considered telling Laurel the whole story...but Laurel's life was complicated enough. The last thing she needed was to hear someone else's troubles.

"Of course not," she said, with a quick smile. "Why on earth would I do that?"

"Good question." Laurel shoved back her chair, rose from the table and stalked to the sink. "If there's one truth in this world," she said, as she turned on the water, "it's that men stink. Oh, not George, Suze. I mean, he's not a man..."

Susie laughed.

"Come on, you know what I'm saying. George is so sweet. He's one in a million."

"I agree," Susie said. She sighed. "And I'd have bet my life your husband was, too."

Laurel swung around, eyes flashing. "I told you, I do not wish to discuss Damian Skouras."

"Well, I know, but you said—"

"Besides, he is not my husband!"

"Well, no, he won't be, after the divorce comes through, but—"

"To hell with that! A man who—who forces a woman into marriage isn't a husband, he's a—a—"

"A no-good, miserable, super-macho stinking son of a bitch, that's what he is!" Annie glared at her sister, as if defying her to disagree. "And don't you tell me you don't want to talk about it, Laurel, because Susie and I have both had just about enough of this nonsense."

"What nonsense? I don't know what you're talk—"

"You damn well *do* know what we're talking about! It's two months now, two whole months since I got that insane call from you, telling me you'd married that—that Greek super-stud and that you'd found him in the arms of his bubble-brained mistress a week later, and in all that time, I'm not supposed to ask any questions or so much as mention his name." Annie folded her arms and lifted her chin. "That is a load of crap, and you know it."

"It isn't." Laurel shut off the water and folded her arms, too. "There's nothing to talk about, Annie."

"Nothing to talk about." Annie snorted. "You got yourself knocked up and let the guy who did it strong-arm you into marrying him!"

Laurel stiffened. "Must you say it like that?"

"It's the truth, isn't it?"

After a minute, Laurel nodded. "I guess it is. God, I almost wish I'd never gone to Dawn's wedding!"

Susie sighed dramatically. "That must have been some

wedding.'' Annie and Laurel spun toward her and she flushed. "Speaking metaphorically, I mean. Hey, come on, guys, don't look at me that way. It must have been one heck of a day. Annie's ex, coming on to her..."

"For all the good it's going to do him," Annie said coldly.

"And didn't you say that friend of yours, Bethany, met some guy there and ended up having a mad affair?"

"Her name's Stephanie, and at the risk of sounding cynical, I don't think very much of mad affairs, not anymore." Annie jerked her chin toward Laurel. "Just look where it got my sister."

"I know." Susie shook her head. "And Damian seemed so perfect. Handsome, rich—"

"Are you two all done discussing me?" Laurel asked. "Because if you aren't, you'll have to continue this conversation elsewhere. I told you, I will not talk about Damian Skouras. That chapter's over and done with."

"Not quite," Annie said, and looked at Laurel's gently rounded belly.

Laurel flushed. "Very amusing."

"Can we at least talk about how you're going to raise this baby all by yourself?"

"I'll manage."

"There are financial implications, dammit. You said yourself you're at the end of your career."

"Thank you for reminding me."

"Laurel, sweetie—"

"Don't 'Laurel sweetie' me. I am a grown woman, and I made a lot of money over the years. Trust me, Annie, I saved quite a bit of it."

"Yes, but children cost. You don't realize—"

"Dammit," Laurel said fiercely, "now you sound just like him!"

"Who?"

"Damian, that's who. Well, you sound like his attorney, anyway. 'Raising a child is an expensive proposition,' she said in a voice that mimicked the rounded tones of John Hastings. "'Mr. Skouras is fully prepared to support his child properly.'"

Susie and Annie exchanged looks. "You never told me that," Susie said.

"Me, neither," Annie added.

Laurel glared at the two women. "It doesn't matter, does it? I'm not about to take a penny from that bastard."

"Yes, but I thought… I mean, I just figured…" Susie cleared her throat. "Not that being willing to support his kid makes me change what I think of the man. Running off that way, going back to his mistress after a week of marriage… It makes me sick just to think about it"

Annie nodded. "You're right. How he could want that idiotic blonde instead of my beautiful sister…"

"He didn't." Susie and Annie looked at Laurel, and she flushed. "I never said that, did I?"

"You said he left you, for the blonde."

"I said he went back to New York and that I found him with her. I never said—"

"So, he didn't want to take up where they'd left off?"

"I don't know what he wanted." Laurel plucked a sponge from the sink, squeezed it dry and began wiping down the counter with a vengeance. "I never gave him the chance to tell me."

"What do you mean, you never…?"

"Look, when you find your husband with a naked blonde, it's not hard to figure what's going on. I just turned around and walked out. Don't look at me like that, Annie. You would have, too."

Annie sighed. "I suppose. What could he possibly have said that would have made things better? Besides, if he'd really wanted to explain, he'd have called you or come to see you—"

"He did come here."

Annie and Susie looked at each other. "He did? When?"

"That same night."

Susie looked shocked. "You see what happens when George and I take a few days off? Laurel, you never said—"

"I wouldn't let him in. What for? We had nothing to say to each other."

"And that was it?" Annie asked. "He gave up, that easily?"

Silence fell on the kitchen and then Laurel cleared her throat.

"He phoned. He left a message on my machine. He said what had happened—what I'd seen—hadn't been what it appeared to be."

"Oh, right," Annie said, "I'll just bet it—"

"What did he say it had been?" Susie asked, shooting Annie a warning look.

"I don't remember," Laurel lied. She remembered every word; she'd listened to Damian's voice a dozen times before erasing it, not just the lying words but the huskiness, hating herself for the memories it stirred in her heart. "Some nonsense about his bimbo threatening to drag my name through the mud unless he paid her off. Oh, what does it matter? He'd have said anything, to get his own way. I told you, he was determined to take my baby."

"Well, it's his baby, too." Susie swallowed hard when both women glared at her. "Well, it is," she said defiantly. "That's just a simple biological fact." She frowned. "Which brings up an interesting point. How come he's backed off?"

Annie frowned, too. "Good question. He has backed off, hasn't he?"

Laurel nodded. She pulled a chair out from the table and sank into it. "Uh-huh. He has."

"How come? Not that I'm not delighted, but why back off now, after first all but dragging you into marriage?"

Laurel folded her hands on the tabletop.

"He—he called and left another message."

"The telephone company's best pal," Susie said brightly.

"He said—he said that he had no right to force me into living with him. That he understood that I could never feel about him as I had about Kirk—"

"Kirk?" Annie's brows arched. "How'd that piece of sewer slime get into the picture?"

"He said he'd been wrong to make me marry him in the first place, that a marriage without love could never work."

"The plot thickens." Susie leaned forward over the table. "I know you guys are liable to tar and feather me for this, but Damian Skouras isn't sounding like quite the scuzzball I'd figured him for."

Annie reached out and clasped her sister's hand. "Maybe you should have taken one of those phone calls, hmm?"

"What for?" Laurel snatched back her hand. "Don't be ridiculous, both of you. I called him and left him a message of my own. I said it didn't matter what had been going on or not going on with the blonde because I agreed completely. Not only could a loveless marriage never work, a marriage in which a wife hated the husband was doomed. And I hated him, I said. I said that I always had, that he had to accept the fact that it had been nothing but sex all along... Don't look at me that way, Annie! What was I supposed to believe? That that woman appeared at his door, uninvited, and stripped off her clothes?"

"Is that what he claimed?"

"Yes!"

Annie smiled gently. "It's possible, isn't it? The lady didn't strike me as the sort given to subtle gestures."

Laurel shot up from her chair. "I don't believe what's going on here! The two of you, asking me to deny what I saw with my own eyes! My God, it was bad enough to be deceived by Kirk, a man I'd thought I loved, but to be deceived by Damian, by my own husband, the only man I've ever really loved, is—is..." Her voice broke. "Oh God, I *do* love him! I'll never stop loving him." She looked from Susie to Annie, and her mouth began to tremble. "Go away," she whispered. "Just go away, and leave me alone."

They didn't, not until Laurel was calmer, not until she was undressed and asleep in her bed.

Then they left because, really, when you came right down to it, what else was there to do?

What else was there to do? Damian thought, as he attacked the boulder outside his house overlooking the Aegean with the sledgehammer.

Nothing. Nothing but beat at this miserable rock and work himself to exhaustion from sunup to sundown in hopes he'd fall into bed at night and not dream of Laurel.

It was a fine plan. Unfortunately it didn't work.

He had not seen Laurel, or heard her voice, in two months—but she was with him every minute of the day, just the same. The nights were even worse. Alone in the darkness, in the bed where he'd once held his wife in his arms, he tossed and turned for hours before falling into restless, dream-filled sleep.

He had considered returning to New York, but he could not imagine himself sitting behind a desk, in the same city where Laurel lived. And so he stayed on Actos, and worked, and sweated, and oversaw his business interests by computer, phone and fax. He told himself that the ache inside him would go away.

It hadn't. If anything, it had grown worse.

He knew that Eleni and Spiro were almost frantic with worry.

"Is he trying to kill himself?" he'd heard Eleni mutter just that morning, as he'd gone out the door. "You must speak to him, Spiro," she'd said.

Damian's mouth thinned as he swung the sledgehammer. If the old man knew what was good for him, he'd keep his mouth shut. He'd interfered enough already. Damian had told him so, on his return to Greece.

"Was it you who permitted my wife to leave the island and follow me to New York?" he'd demanded.

Spiro had stiffened. "*Né*," he'd said, "yes, it was I."

Damian's hands had balled into fists. "On whose authority did you do this thing, old man?"

"On my own," Spiro had replied quietly. "The woman was not a prisoner here."

A muscle had knotted in Damian's cheek. "No," he'd said, "she was not."

Spiro had waited before speaking again.

"She said that she had something of great importance to tell you," he'd said, his eyes on Damian's. "Did she find you, and deliver her message?"

Damian's mouth had twisted. "She did, indeed," he'd replied, and when Spiro had tried to say more, he'd held up his hand. "There is nothing to discuss. The woman is not to be mentioned again."

She had not been, to this day. But that didn't mean he didn't think about her, and dream about her. Did she dream of him? Did she ever long for the feel of his arms and the sweetness of his kisses, as he longed for hers?

Did she ever think of how close they'd come to happiness?

Damian's throat constricted. He swung the hammer hard, but his aim wasn't true. His vision was blurred—by sweat, for what else could it be?—and the hammer hit the rock a glancing blow.

"Dammit," he growled, and swung again.

"Damian," Spiro's voice was soft. "The rock is not your enemy."

"And you are not a philosopher," Damian snapped, and swung again.

"What you battle is not the boulder, my son, it is yourself."

Damian straightened up. "Listen here," he said, but his anger faded when he looked at the old man. Spiro looked exhausted. Sweat stained his dark trousers and shirt; his weathered face was bright red and there was a tremor in his hands.

Why was the old fool so stubborn? The heat was too much for a man his age. Damian sighed, set the sledgehammer aside and stripped off his work gloves.

"It is hot," he said. "I need something to drink."

"There is a bottle of *retsina* in my jacket, under the tree."

Damian plucked his discarded T-shirt from the ground and slipped it on.

"I know the sort of *retsina* you drink, old man. The sun will rot our brains quickly enough, without its help. We will go up to the house. Perhaps we can convince Eleni to give us some cold beer."

"*Né.*" Spiro smiled. "For once, you have an excellent idea."

It took no convincing at all. Eleni took one look at them, rolled her eyes and brought cold beer and glasses out to the terrace. Damian ignored the glasses, handed one bottle to the old man and took the other for himself. He leaned back against the railing and took a long drink. Spiro drank, too, then wiped his mustache with the back of his hand.

"When do you return to New York?" he said.

Damian's brows lifted. "Are you in such a rush to get rid of me?"

"You cannot avoid reality forever, Damian."

"Spiro." Damian's voice was chill. "I warn you, do not say anything more. It is hot, I am in a bad mood—"

"As if that were anything new."

Damian tilted the beer bottle to his lips. He drank, then set the bottle down. "I am going back to work. I suggest you go inside, where it is cooler."

"I suggest you stop pretending you do not have a wife."

"I told you, we will not discuss her."

"And now I tell you that we must."

"Dammit, old man—"

"I saw how happy she made you, Damian, and how happy you made her."

"Are you deaf? I said that we would not—"

"You loved her. And you love her still."

"No! No, I do not love her. What is love anyway, but a thing to make men idiots?"

Spiro chuckled and folded his arms. "Are you saying I was an idiot to put up with you, after I found you on the streets of Athens? Be careful, or I will have to take a switch to your backside, as I did when you were a boy."

"You know what I mean," Damian said, stubbornly refusing to be taken in. "I'm talking of male and female love, and I tell you that I did not *love* her. All right? Are you satisfied now? Can I get back to work?"

"She loved you."

"Never." Damian's voice roughened. "She did not love me, old man. She despised me for everything I am and especially for forcing her into a marriage she did not want."

"She loved you," Spiro repeated. "I know this, for a fact."

"She loved another, you sentimental old fool."

"It is not sentiment or foolishness that makes me say this, Damian, it is the knowledge of what she told me."

Damian's face went pale beneath its tan. "What the hell are you talking about?"

"It is the reason I sent her after you. She said she loved you deeply."

For one sweet instant, Damian felt his heart might burst from his chest. But then he remembered the reality of what had happened: the swiftness with which Laurel had accepted the ugly scene orchestrated by Gabriella, the way she'd refused even to listen to his explanation…and the message he'd found on his answering machine, Laurel's cool voice saying that she'd never stopped hating him, that what they'd shared had been nothing but sex…

"You misunderstood her, old man. You speak English almost as badly as she spoke Greek."

"I know what she told me, Damian."

"Then she lied," Damian said coldly. He picked up the bottle and drained it dry. "She lied, because it was the only way she could get you to agree to let her leave the island, and you fell for it. Now, I am going to work and you are going to stay out of the sun before it bakes your brain completely. Is that clear?"

"What is clear," the old man said quietly, "is that I raised a coward."

Damian spun toward him, his eyes gone hard and chill. "If any other man but you dared say such a thing to me," he said softly, "I would beat him within an inch of his life."

"You are a coward in your heart, afraid to face the truth. You love this woman but because she hurt you in some fashion, you would rather live your life without her than risk going after her."

"Damn you to hell," Damian roared, and thrust his face into the old man's. "Listen, Spiro, and listen well, for I will say this only once. Yes, I love her. But she does not love me."

"How do you know this?"

"How? How?" Damian's teeth glinted in a hollow laugh. "She told me so, all right? Does that satisfy you?"

"Did you ever tell her that you loved her?"

"Did I ever...?" Damian threw his arms skyward. "By all the gods that be, I cannot believe this! No, I never told her. She never gave me the chance. She came bursting into my apartment in New York, found me with another woman and damned me without even giving me an opportunity to explain."

Spiro's weather-beaten face gave nothing away. "And what were you doing with this woman, my son? Arranging flowers, perhaps?"

Damian colored. "I admit, it did not look good..."

"You were not arranging flowers?"

"What is this? An interrogation? I had just come out of the shower, okay? And the woman—the woman was trying to seduce me. I just admitted, it did not look good." He took a deep breath. "But Laurel is my wife. She should have trusted me."

"Certainly she should have trusted you. After all, what had you ever done to make her distrustful, except to impregnate her and force her into a marriage she did not want?"

"How did you—"

"Eleni says that there is a look to a woman's face, when she is carrying a child. Any fool could see it, just as any fool could see that when you first brought her here, neither of you was happy." Spiro smiled. "But that changed, Damian. I do not know how it happened, but you both finally admitted what had been in your hearts from the beginning."

"All right. Yes, I fell in love with her. But nothing is that simple."

"Love is never simple."

Damian turned and clasped the railing. He could feel his anger seeping away and a terrible despair replacing it.

"Spiro, you are the father I never knew and I trust your advice, you know that, but in this matter—"

"In this matter, Damian," the old man said, "trust your heart. Go to her, tell her that you love her. Give her the chance to tell you the same thing."

Damian's throat felt tight. He blinked his eyes, which seemed suddenly damp.

"And if she does not?" he said gruffly. "What then?"

"Then you will return here and swing that hammer until your arms ache with the effort—but you will return knowing that you tried to win the woman you love instead of letting her slip away." Spiro put his hand on Damian's shoulder. "There is always hope, my son. It is that which gives us the will to go on, né?"

Out in the bay, a tiny sailboat heeled under the wind. The sea reached up for it with greedy, white-tipped fingers. Surely it would be swallowed whole...

The wind subsided as quickly as it had begun. The boat bobbed upright.

There is always hope.

Quickly, before he could lose his courage, Damian turned and embraced the old man. Then he headed into the house.

They were wrong. Dead wrong.

Laurel pounded furiously at the lump of sourdough.

What did Annie and Susie know, anyway? Annie was divorced and Susie was married to a marshmallow. Neither of them had ever had the misfortune to deal with a macho maniac like Damian Skouras.

Damn, but it was hot! Too hot for making bread but what else was she going to do with all this pent-up energy? Laurel blew a strand of hair out of her eyes, wiped her hand over her nose and began beating the dough again.

They were driving her crazy, her sister and her friend. Ever since yesterday, when she'd been dumb enough to break down in front of them and admit she'd loved Damian, they hadn't left her alone. If it wasn't Annie phoning, it was Susie.

Well, let 'em phone. She'd given up answering. Let the machine deal with the cheery "hi"'s and the even cheerier "Laurel? Are you there, honey?"'s.

This morning, in a fit of pique, she'd snatched up the phone, snarled, "No, I'm not there, *honey*," and slammed it down again before Annie or Susie, whichever it was, could say a word. Why listen to either of them, when she knew what they were going to say? They'd both said it already, that maybe she'd misjudged Damian, that maybe what he'd told her about the blonde was the truth.

"I didn't," Laurel muttered, picking up the dough and then slamming it down again. "And it wasn't."

And anyway, what did it matter? So what, if maybe, just maybe, Blondie had set him up? He'd left her, damn him, in the middle of the honeymoon, he'd gone off without a word.

Because you hurt him, Laurel, have you forgotten that?

No, she thought grimly, no, she had not forgotten. So she'd hurt him. Big deal. He'd hurt her a heck of a lot more, not telling her where he was going or even that he was going, not saying goodbye...

Not loving her, when she loved him so terribly that she couldn't shut her eyes without seeing his face or hearing his voice or—

"Laurel?"

Like that. Exactly like that. She could hear him say her name, as if he were right here, in the room with her...

"Laurel, *mátya mou*..."

Laurel spun around, and her heart leaped into her throat. "Damian?"

Damian cursed as her knees buckled. He rushed forward, caught her in his arms and carried her into the living room. "Take a deep breath," he ordered, as he sat down on the sofa with her still in his arms. "You're not going to pass out on me, are you?"

"Of course not," she said, when the mist before her eyes cleared away. "I never pass out."

"No," he said wryly, "you never do—except at the sight of me."

"What are you going here, Damian? And how did you get in?"

"That George," he said, smoothing the hair back from her face with his hand. "What a splendid fellow he is."

"George gave you my spare key? Dammit, he had no right! *You* had no—"

"And I see that I got here just in time." A smile tilted at the corner of his mouth. "You've been doing experiments in the kitchen again."

"I've been making bread. And don't try to change the

subject. You had absolutely no right to unlock the door and—''

"I know, and I apologize. But I was afraid that you'd leave me standing in the hall again, if I asked you to let me in.''

"You're right, I would have done exactly that.'' Laurel put her hands on his shoulders. "Let me up, please.''

"I love you, Laurel.''

Hope flickered in her heart, but fear snuffed it out.

"You just want your child,'' she said.

"I want *our* child, my darling wife, but more than that, I want you. I love you, Laurel.'' He took her face in his hands. "I adore you,'' he said softly. "You're the only woman I have ever loved, the only woman I will ever love, and if you don't come back to me, I will be lost forever.''

Tears roses in Laurel's eyes. "Oh, Damian. Do you mean it?''

He kissed her. It was a long, sweet, wonderful kiss, and when it ended, she was trembling.

"With all my heart. I should have awakened you that night and told you I had to leave, but you were so angry and I—I was angry, too, and wounded by the knowledge that you'd once loved another.''

Laurel shook her head. "I didn't love him. I only talked about Kirk to hurt you. I've never loved anyone, until you.''

"Tell me again,'' he whispered.

She smiled. "I love you, Damian. I've never loved anyone else. I never will. There's only you, only you, only—''

He kissed her again, then leaned his forehead against hers.

"What I told you about Gabriella was the truth. I didn't ask her to my apartment. She—''

Laurel kissed him to silence. A long time later, Damian drew back.

"We'll fly to Actos,'' he said, "and ask that interfering old man to drink champagne with us.''

Laurel linked her arms around her husband's neck and smiled into his eyes.

"Did anybody ever tell you that you can sound awfully arrogant at times?"

Damian grinned as he got to his feet with his wife in his arms.

"Someone might have mentioned it, once or twice," he said, as he shouldered open the bedroom door.

Laurel's pulse quickened as he slowly lowered her to the bed.

"I thought we were going to Actos," she whispered.

"We are." Damian gave her a slow, sexy kiss. "But first," he said, as he began to undo her buttons, "first, we've got to get reacquainted."

Laurel sighed as he slipped off her blouse. "And how long do you think that's going to take, husband?"

Damian smiled. "All the rest of our lives, wife."

Slowly he gathered her into his arms.

EPILOGUE

No one on the island of Actos had ever seen anything quite like it.

There were always weddings, of course, young people and life being as they are, but even the old women at the fish market, who usually argued about everything, agreed on this.

There had never been a wedding the equal of Damian and Laurel's.

Of course, as the old women were quick to point out, the Skourases were already married. But the ceremony that had joined them meant nothing. It had been performed all the way across the sea, in America, and—can you imagine?—a judge had said the words that had made them man and wife, not a priest.

No wonder they had chosen to be wed all over again, and in the proper way.

The day was perfect: a clear blue sky, a peaceful sea, and though the sun shone brightly, it was not too hot.

The bride, the old ladies said, was beautiful in her lacy white gown. And oh, her smile. So radiant, so filled with love for her handsome groom.

Handsome, indeed, one of the crones said, and she added something else behind her wrinkled hand that made them all cackle with delight.

It was just too bad the bride wasn't Greek...but she was the next best thing. Beautiful, with shining eyes and a bright smile, and Eleni had told them that she was learning to think like one of them, enough so that when her groom had teasingly warned her that marriage in a Greek church was forever, she'd smiled and put her arms around him and said that was the only kind of marriage she'd ever wanted.

And so, in a little church made of whitewashed stone, with the sun streaming through the windows and baskets of flowers banked along the aisle and at the altar, and with friends and relatives from faraway America flown over for this most special of days, Laurel Bennett and Damian Skouras were wed.

"Yes," Laurel said clearly, when the priest asked—in English, at Damian's request—if she would take the man beside her as her husband, to love and honor and cherish for the rest of her days. And when Damian offered the same pledge, he broke with tradition by looking deep into his wife's eyes and saying that he would cherish forever the woman he had waited all his life to find.

The old ladies in black wept, as did the two stylishly dressed American women in the front pew. Even old Spiro wiped his eyes, though he said later that it was only because a speck had gotten into one.

Retsina and *ouzo* flowed, and bubbly champagne flown in from France. Everyone danced, and sang; they ate lobster and red snapper and roast lamb, and the men toasted the bride and groom until none could think of another reason to raise his glass.

It was, everyone said, an absolutely wonderful wedding—but if you'd asked the bride and the groom what part was the most wonderful, they'd have said it came late that night, when the crickets were singing and the air was heavy with the scent of flowers and they were alone, at last, on their hilltop overlooking the sea.

The groom took his bride in his arms.

"You are my heart," he said, looking deep into her eyes, and she smiled so radiantly that his heart almost shattered with joy.

"As you are mine," she whispered, and as the ivory moon climbed into the black velvet sky, Damian swept Laurel into his arms and carried her up to their bedroom.

*   *   *

The next morning, Laurel awoke to the ring of the sledge-hammer.

She dressed quickly and went outside, to where the boulder stood.

"Damian," she called, and her husband turned and smiled at her.

"Watch," he said.

He swung the hammer against the boulder. The sound rang like a bell across the hilltop, and the rock crumbled into a thousand tiny pieces.

Catch more great
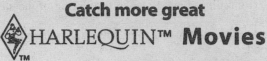
HARLEQUIN™ Movies

featured on the movie channel tmc

Premiering May 9th
The Awakening

starring Cynthia Geary and
David Beecroft, based on the novel by
Patricia Coughlin

Don't miss next month's movie!
Premiering June 13th
Diamond Girl
based on the novel by bestselling author
Diana Palmer

If you are not currently a subscriber to
The Movie Channel, simply call your
local cable or satellite provider for more
details. Call today, and don't miss out
on the romance!

100% pure movies.
100% pure fun.

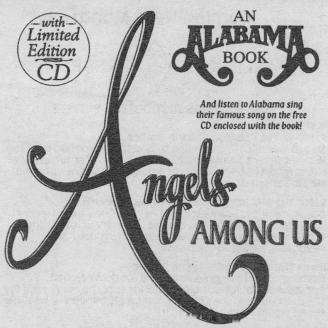
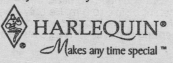

Coming Next Month